Fallen For You

SYLVER MICHAELA

Fallen for You by Sylver Michaela

ISBN: 978-0-578-63414-2

Prologue

MY FEET THUDDED AGAINST the ground as I ran deeper into the woods. Tears streamed down my face, and I wiped at them angrily. I shouldn't have been crying. I was sixteen. You didn't cry at sixteen. Plus, I should be used to his behavior by now. It was all I'd ever known. I needed to grow up and accept the fact that my dad was a drunk who didn't care.

But I didn't want to accept it, so I kept running. Branches scratched at my arms and legs the farther I ran, but I ignored them. I just wanted to make it to my special place. Pushing forward, I emerged through a group of naked branches and stepped into the clearing.

My clearing.

It was a wide open space, surrounded by trees. There was a shallow, crystal blue pond in the center with patches of grass scattered around it. Small rays of sunlight shone through the branches of the trees causing a golden light to fill my sanctuary. I stepped forward and chose the small bed of clovers next to the water. It was the same spot I always used as my seat.

Slowly sitting down, I peeked into the water, and my red blotchy face looked back at me. Another tear escaped, gradually falling towards the water. When it hit the surface, ripples blurred my reflection. I looked up and leaned back on my hands while taking deep, slow breaths. I shut my eyes and willed the pain to go away.

I wanted peace of mind. I wanted a dad who didn't drink from his every waking moment until the time he passed out. I wanted a mom who didn't just walk out before her own daughter was even old enough to speak. I wanted someone to share happy memories with, someone I could hold close to my heart.

Opening my eyes, I looked around at my little haven. I came here so often because it was the only place I felt safe. It was the only place I felt something other than desperation and loneliness. I'd never been able to explain why, but here it felt like someone was watching over me, someone who did care.

When I was little, I would pretend there was someone here with me whom I talked to. I would laugh with this imaginary friend, and he or she - I never did figure out what gender I thought it might be - would laugh with me, making everything okay. It was just the two of us, and the problems at home didn't exist. Here, I was happy.

I remained rooted to that spot as the sun started to set. I didn't want to go back to the misery that waited for me at home. Only after the shadows turned dark did I decide it was time to leave. Sighing, I prepared to go back when I felt a warm, tingling sensation on my left hand. I looked down to see what was touching me, but nothing was there.

Looking into the empty space next to me, I thought about my imaginary childhood friend again. I pictured the possibility of them sitting next to me, looking at me, and holding my hand just to reassure me that everything was going to be okay. But I wasn't a child anymore, so I knew better.

I turned back to the water and noticed a discolored portion of the pond out of the corner of my eye. My breath left me when I caught a glimpse of what appeared to be a glowing outline of someone sitting next to me. It was a faint white glow that resembled starlight. I quickly rubbed my eyes and looked back. The glow was gone. My eyes traveled back to the empty space next to me. Nothing.

I shook my head as I rationalized the incident as my mind playing tricks on me. Reluctantly, I prepared to stand up when a twig snapped to my left. I jerked my head in that direction, my heart catching in my throat as icy fear shot through me. A large, black wolf was standing at the edge of my clearing, watching me with piercing blue eyes. As I stared back at him, my heart picked up it's pace. I didn't dare try to move because if I did and he decided to chase me, I knew I'd never make it. I hoped that if I remained still, he would leave.

As I watched him cautiously, he took a small step towards me. I swallowed hard and clenched my eyes shut, too afraid to open them again. My body shook slightly as the terror ran through me, and I willed myself to sit completely still. I waited and prayed for him to be gone when I opened my eyes, but when I felt a warm breath hitting my cheek, I knew he wasn't going anywhere.

Opening my eyes again, I found the large creature sitting next to me. Gazing into his crystal blue eyes, I silently cried. I knew this would be my last moment on earth, but part of me was almost glad. I was tired of living a life without family, friends, or any sort of real affection. Maybe it was best to die in my sacred place.

Just when I thought death was about to come, the beautiful creature closed his eyes and leaned forward to press his forehead against mine. He rested his soft, cool fur against my face, and almost against my will, my fear actually subsided. My body loosened, and I let out the shaky breath I had been holding. I didn't know what was happening or why I was no longer afraid, but I just knew this animal was not here to hurt me.

I closed my eyes, letting him rest his forehead against mine. All the pain and exhaustion I had been feeling suddenly left me as a feeling of love and protection surrounded me. A tear rolled down my cheek, and the large beast pulled back slightly to wipe it away with his snout.

I looked back into his eyes as he stared into mine. It was hard to believe I was actually facing a wolf like this. I had no idea if I was dreaming by this point or if this was really happening. Either way, this moment was something incredible and unforgettable. This moment was a gift from God.

"Thank you," I whispered to him. I knew he wouldn't be able to understand, but I needed to say it. I needed the words to come out and tie me to this moment. This magnificent being had been like a light in all the darkness around me. I didn't know how this was possible, but I was thankful for this experience.

He dipped his head, as though he were nodding. He got to his feet, his fluffy tail flicking behind him as he turned to leave. I watched him walk back into the trees, taking that blanket of warmth and safety with him. My body remained frozen to the spot for a few more moments. I was having trouble believing what just happened.

I couldn't wrap my head around the fact that this wolf seemed to be comforting me. Things like this just weren't possible. I didn't need to stick around here any longer though. He may have been tame, but if there were more wolves around, I didn't want to stay to find out. I stood up and made my way back to the home I so desperately hated.

The trailer my dad and I lived in had numerous broken windows with garbage bags taped over them, which didn't always work to keep the cold out. Not having enough money to install new glass panes, multiple blankets became our way of staying warm. Trash littered every part of the outside, and when I would attempt to clean it, my dad would find ways to create more filth. It was a terrible place to call home, so I never did. It was nothing more than a place that caused pain.

The clearing was my only true happy place - or at least it was until the next time I went back. I didn't feel that same presence of tenderness and shelter after that day. It was as if when that wolf left, he took all the light from it too. I felt cold, afraid, and abandoned when I tried going back. Whatever had been there before, whether it was my imaginary friend or the wolf, was gone. It made me feel discarded and on my own, so I never went back after that.

I decided I would find a new way to escape from my dad and my life in that trailer; however, I still hoped that maybe one day I could go back to find that the warm presence had returned. Whether that be my imaginary friend or the wolf, I didn't care. Maybe it would happen tomorrow. Maybe in a couple of years. It didn't matter when. I just hoped for the day I'd find that feeling again.

One day.

Someday.

Chapter One

Two Years Later

I GROANED AS I tugged on my jacket over my orange and white waitress uniform. It was fifteen minutes until 6 a.m., the time my shift started. I yawned as I fought the persistent urge to climb back into my warm bed. No matter how tempting the idea seemed, I knew I couldn't. I needed this job, as well as my other two, since I was the only source of income for me and my dad.

Pulling my shiny black curls into a high ponytail, I walked out of my room towards the front door. My dad's snoring could be heard all the way down the hall, and once I reached the living room, I saw him slumped down in his aged recliner. His white shirt was barely covering his beer gut, and it was stained with the alcohol he'd let fall from his hand during his sleep.

I was exhausted, so I just sighed and rolled my eyes. As

I worked to pick up the dozens of bottles around his recliner, he shifted in his drunken sleep. This was normal for me. He spent every day drowning himself in whiskey and beer, so I was used to this sort of thing. I couldn't even remember the last time I saw him sober.

I walked into our small kitchen and placed the bottles in the sink to deal with later. I didn't feel like fooling with them now, and I needed to get to work. Making my way back into the living room, I made an attempt at slowly prying away the bottle he still held out of his hand. This caused him to stir, and his eyes slowly fluttered open.

He blinked a couple of times as I finally got the bottle away from him. When he was somewhat conscious, he looked into my hand and sneered at me. "What the hell do you think you're doing?"

"It's empty, Dad. I'm taking it to the sink." I kept my voice level. Using any other tone with him would result in a battle I didn't have time for.

Turning, I walked back into the dark kitchen. I tossed the bottle in the sink and heard him grumbling behind me. Sighing, I made my way towards the front door, where my bag waited.

"Where are you going?" my dad questioned with his eyes already fluttering shut. He was no doubt falling back asleep. "Where's my beer?"

"You don't need a beer. You're sleeping. And I'm going to work."

I stood next to his chair as I hauled my bag onto my shoulder with a heavy sigh. I leaned down to kiss his forehead, but he only groaned and shoved me away. I was forced to scrunch my nose as a tight grip formed in my throat. I couldn't cry. I wouldn't cry.

"I love you, Dad."

"Whatever." He turned his head away, snoring once more.

His rejection didn't hurt as much as it used to. Turns out that when you get hurt enough, you just become numb to the pain. That was how our relationship was now. He was numb to reality, and I was numb to his insults.

When I stepped outside, I was greeted by the cold, but I embraced it in hopes that it would freeze any emotions I had left. I made my way towards town, feeling the tip of my nose burn the further I walked in the brisk air. Holding the strap of my bag to keep it from falling, I looked down at my feet as I became lost in my chaotic thoughts. That's when I heard a twig snap to my right.

My stomach curled in knots as I turned towards the woods. It was still semi-dark out, so I couldn't see anything past all of the tall trees. I walked this path to work and school every day, and the woods never really bothered me, not even at night. Today however there was something eerie about its shadows and dancing limbs. The wind blowing through the branches made it sound like hushed whispers were coming from somewhere in the darkness.

Narrowing my eyes, I tried to peer further into the obscurity of the forest. It was most likely just an animal walking around somewhere, but my nerves were still on edge. I didn't feel like standing alone in the dark anymore, so I pulled my bag close to me as I jogged the rest of the way to the diner.

The Night Light Diner sat at the edge of town along the main road, which connected to the interstate and highways. It was a place for truckers to stop and eat at any time of the day or night because it was open 24/7. The shifts were divided up between 10 of us. I worked from 6 a.m. to 11 a.m. on weekends.

When I walked in, the bell above the door rang, causing Gloria to look up at me from behind the counter.

"Mornin' Miss Raven," she said.

Gloria's southern accent filled my ears. She was a kind, Christian, black woman who was always friendly towards me. She was one of the few people who seemed to notice me or my feelings, which meant a lot. Even though she was much older than me, I was closer to her than any other person in my life.

"Good morning," I said, moving behind the counter. I took off my bag and jacket and placed them in a cubby under the bar. "What time did you get here?"

"Few minutes ago." She sipped her coffee while staring blankly at the TV in the corner. The news was on, as usual. I tied my apron around my waist and looked into the kitchen. "Good morning, Freddie." I waved at the old man, and he grunted in response. He wasn't really a morning person.

I turned away just as the bell rang. A man with a long beard and braid came in. He sported a pair of faded jeans and an old black t-shirt. As he sat down at a booth near the television, I approached him with a smile. "Can I get you anything?"

"Uhh," he scanned the very small menu then looked at me. He returned my friendly smile and said, "Scrambled eggs, bacon, sausage, and black coffee."

I took the menu from him. "Alrighty."

I walked back to the counter to give Freddie the order before grabbing the coffee pot. Striding back over to the strangers booth, I sat his mug down and began filling it with the rich, black brew, when a woman's voice rang out from the television.

"A devastating event has occurred here in Smitherson. A young boy by the name of Brendon Hillock was murdered last night in a deserted alley. The police-"

"Wow," Gloria said, staring wide eyed at the screen. "Lord be with that family right now."

"That's awful!" I looked back at the TV. "Why would somebody do that?"

"World's a dark place. People are cruel, and they don't think about the results of their actions." She shook her head then asked, "Did you know him?"

Looking back at her, I shook my head. "He goes to my- or I guess went to my school. Everyone knew Brendon. He was the star athlete there, but I didn't know him personally."

The man I had been attending to cleared his throat and said, "Sorry about your town's loss."

I looked at him and gave him a smile that didn't quite reach my eyes. Even though I didn't know Brendon, I still couldn't imagine the horror he must have felt. Looking back at the TV, I wondered who would have murdered him. Was it an attack that had been specific to him, or did we have a new killer dwelling amongst us?

I swallowed hard. My heart wrenched for Brendon and those close to him. How was one even supposed to cope with news like that? My guess was you didn't. I couldn't even begin to fathom how this must be affecting his family and friends. My stomach coiled up at the thought of what his last moments alive must have been like. There was probably screaming, crying, terror. Pain.

My legs felt shaky with all the emotions running through me, so I walked over to the counter and sat down at one of the bar stools. Letting out a deep breath, I tried calming myself down.

"Don't worry, Raven." Gloria patted me on the shoulder. "Ain't nobody gonna touch you."

I nodded before the customer said, "I don't know. I'd be careful just in case. No walking around alone when it's dark out."

I closed my eyes and did my best to ignore his warning. I tried to push away my growing anxiety, which stemmed from knowing a killer was nearby. Things like this had never happened here before, so this unfamiliar incident was causing me to panic. When my eyes found their way back to the TV screen, it was showing pictures of the crime scene.

Brendon was lying face down behind a dumpster with a cloth draped over his body. I swallowed and began to feel nauseated at the thought of what his body now looked like underneath that cloth. I turned away from the TV, and suddenly, I couldn't wait for daylight.

***

At 10:55, I sorted through my tips. The morning had been slow, and all I had was $8 and some change. I put the money in my wallet and grabbed my stuff.

"Hey Gloria, do you mind if I head out early? Mrs. Morea wants me to open shop while she sorts through packages that arrived."

"Yeah honey, go'on. Be careful." She slid a man a plate of food then gave me a wide smile. I knew what that grin actually meant. *Don't worry. You'll be fine.* I just returned her hidden message with a slight nod.

On my way to the door, I overheard two men discussing Brendon, who had made it onto the cover of our newspaper. Hearing them discuss the murder made me uneasy, so when I stepped out into the chilly September weather, my goosebumps weren't just from the cold. I swallowed down my nerves and made my way to the bookstore. I couldn't help but look around me at all times. Despite the sun being out, people walking past me, and cars roaring by, I was still shaken up.

A murderer. In my town. He could be anywhere.

He could be right behind me.

Speeding up my pace, I finally arrived at the bookstore to find a very irritated Mrs. Morea.

"You're late," she said, glaring at me with her hands poised on both hips.

I looked at my watch. 11:01. She was always very harsh

and never missed even the smallest things. She was constantly getting onto me for things like stacking the papers on the counter without ensuring they were completely straight, or she would say that my shirt had too many wrinkles so I needed to fetch a new one. Mrs. Morea was a proper old lady, and she expected that of me too. No mistakes, no exceptions.

"I'm so sorry. I was at the diner and-"

She held up one wrinkly hand and said, "Spare me your excuses." Unlocking the door, she made her way to the back of the store. I walked in after her, shutting the door behind me.

"You aren't the only late one," she huffed. "That damn mailman hasn't come with my packages yet. No matter. You will handle it when he arrives. I'm headed out to lunch, then I have to go to the hospital to see my new grandchild."

I smiled and said, "Congra-"

"I need you to lock up tonight since I will be busy."

My stomach dropped at her command. Wringing my hands, I debated what to do. I wanted to argue with her because I was nervous to stay here late and walk home in the dark after learning about Brendon. Mrs. Morea wasn't someone that was easy to talk back to, but I really didn't want to stay here alone like that.

I held my breath as she reached the door. Before she walked out, I mustered up all of my courage and said, "Actually Mrs. Morea, I was hoping I could get off before nightfall. That boy being killed last night has me freaked out. I don't want to walk home in the dark."

She rolled her eyes and said, "Don't flatter yourself,

Raven. No one would waste their time killing you. Murderers like to harm people who are important so that they'll get recognition. They want to make headlines in the news. Killing star athletes who are meant to make it in the big world outside of a small town like ours will definitely be noticed. You're not anyone important like that. So see? You're safe. Don't forget to lock up tonight."

And with that, she left. Slowly sitting down on the chair behind the checkout counter, I let out a painful sigh. She was right. I wasn't important. I wasn't someone like Brendon who would be missed. I didn't have any meaning to anyone, so my being gone wouldn't matter. That meant a murderer wouldn't waste their time on me. Despite the news that I was most likely not in danger, her words brought me no comfort. They only hurt me more.

I headed to the back bathroom to change out of my diner uniform and pulled on my jeans and sweatshirt. When I came back down the hall and sat down in my chair, the door opened. A young man wearing dark jeans and a black t-shirt came in. He was tall and wellbuilt with broad shoulders. He had a nicely trimmed beard, and he wore his long black hair in a bun. His eyes were a deep brown, so much so that they almost appeared black. Everything about him screamed mysterious, which put me slightly on edge.

"Hi there," he said smoothly, slowly approaching the counter. He smiled at me, making his dark eyes crinkle at the sides.

"Hi," I said as I attempted to swallow my nerves. "Can I help you find something?"

"Yes, actually." He looked around and said, "Do you sell the paper here?"

I pointed towards the far end of the counter, where a stack of the morning paper laid. He smiled even broader at me and grabbed one. He looked at the front page where the story of Brendon was already printed. I'm sure his killer was proud. He had made front page news, even if his name wasn't mentioned. His work was on display for everyone to see.

"Terrible story. Of that kid." He glanced at me then continued reading the paper. "Isn't exactly a great first impression for us new folks in town."

"You're new here?" I asked. My nerves were finally calming down. The longer he stood there, the easier it became to interact with him. It was as if the dark aura that entered with him had receded back. He no longer made me feel uneasy, which puzzled me. Nothing had changed.

He smiled. "I am. My brother and I just moved here."

He nodded towards the door. My gaze traveled to where he gestured, and my heart fluttered slightly. A guy who looked about my age was leaning against the door frame outside. He was taller than me, but shorter than his brother. His body was slender yet built at the same time. He was staring off away from us, his obsidian hair moving as the wind blew. His lips were pursed, as though he were in deep thought. My knees grew weak at the sight of him. I had never seen anyone as gorgeous as him.

I could sense my cheeks growing red, so I looked away from him and back to the man in front of me. Breathing in and out slowly, I calmed my racing heart. I had no idea why

I was reacting this way. It was just a boy.

A very attractive boy.

"Well, welcome to Smitherson. I'm Raven." I held out my hand, and he shook it with a smile.

"Landon," he greeted.

"Nice to meet you." I smiled back.

He pointed to the paper in his hand and asked, "How much?"

"Just a dollar."

Lying the newspaper down on the counter, he got out his wallet. As he searched for a dollar, I stole another glance at his brother standing outside. He looked sideways in my direction, and I quickly averted my eyes back to Landon, who handed me the dollar.

"Thank you." I wondered if he could hear the nervousness in my voice.

"No, thank you." He smiled. I held my breath and didn't let it go until he was out of the door.

Releasing my breath with a heavy sigh, I opened the cash register to put the money in. I was still looking down when I heard the door open again. Raising my head up to greet the customer, I froze when I saw *him.* He was walking towards me, his face expressionless. My heart began pounding against my chest, and I knew I was blushing like a fool.

Stopping in front of me, he grabbed the newspaper that Landon must've left behind. He held it up. "Forgot to grab it."

I didn't know what to do. The sound of his deep, rich

voice had my own caught in my throat. Afraid my voice wouldn't work, I just nodded. He turned to walk out when something deep inside my chest forced me to blurt, "Hi!" As soon as the word left my mouth, I silently cursed myself. I sounded like an idiot.

At the sound of me speaking, he stopped walking. He didn't face me. He merely glanced over his shoulder.

I took a deep breath and decided to keep talking since I had already started. "I'm- I'm Raven." His hand was on the doorknob, but he didn't move to open it. He just stood there, listening to me sound foolish. "Your brother said you guys were new in town. I just wanted to say welcome to-"

He turned the knob and walked out, not bothering to listen any longer. I didn't blame him. I sounded lame, but still, my heart sunk. My eyes followed him as he slipped into the driver's side of their car and drove off.

The sight of him leaving, despite not knowing him at all, left me feeling oddly alone and disappointed. I couldn't explain why, but his cold attitude hurt me more than it probably should have. My chest was tight, and there was a knot in my throat. Why did his rejection hurt this bad?

Chapter Two

"THANKS. HAVE A GOOD night," I said as I put the girl's money in the cash register.

"You too," she said. She sauntered to the door and left. I sighed when the door shut behind her and looked at my watch. It was nearly nine, which meant it was time to close up.

I went through the motions of shutting everything down for the night. Part of me was happy to be done with work, but waves of anxiety swept through me as I dreaded the moment when I had to walk out into the dark night. Once I finally completed all of my tasks, I made a point to gather my belongings slowly just to buy more time. I needed to calm down before I tried to go outside. After all, there was probably nothing to be afraid of. I was just overreacting.

Mustering up all of my courage, I stepped into the brisk night air and faced the dark, deserted sidewalk. Gulping down my nerves, I started towards home.

Since it was late at night, the only places really open

were the bars and the diner, which was a few blocks away. With no one out on the streets, I was forced to walk alone, which made my stomach drop and my heart pound. I hugged my arms around myself and attempted to rub away the chills I felt. My eyes searched all around in the darkness for anything out of the ordinary. I was terrified of what could be hiding in the shadows.

I kept casting glances in every direction. My palms grew sweaty as I neared an alley. The amount of fear and paranoia coursing through me had me on the verge of being sick. The only thing I could picture was Brendon's mutilated body lying face down on the ground. I didn't want that to be me. I didn't want to die. I rushed past the entrance of the alley, and when I made it past safely, I let out a sigh of relief. Looking back, I giggled.

"Raven, you are beyond paranoid," I muttered to myself.

I walked a few more steps, feeling braver and more confident when, all of a sudden, I felt someone's hands wrap around my mouth and body. Terror instantly shot through me as I was pulled against them and drug back into the alley. The scream I wanted to cry boiled up inside of me as I fought to let it out. Their hand was wrapped too tightly around my mouth for any sound to have a chance of coming out.

My heart was pounding, and tears streamed down my cheeks. My attacker's stomach and chest were pressed against my back so hard, it almost hurt. They were panting in my ear as I fought against their hold. I kept jerking from side to side, trying to wiggle my body loose from their grip. If only

I could break free for just a moment, maybe I could get away. Maybe I could cry for help. There was a bar not too far down the street. Maybe someone would hear.

The thought gave me enough will to kick harder and beat my fists against the person's legs. Their breath came out hard near my ear as they struggled to keep their hold on me while also trying to drag me further into the dark. Their grip was turning sweaty against my mouth, which allowed me to pry my lips apart just enough to bite their hand. I bit down hard into their flesh, and they jerked their hand away quickly. A deep, male voice uttered a curse, and he squeezed his arm tighter around me. Despite his solid grip around my frame, I took the opportunity to send out a blood-curdling cry.

"Shit!" he hissed.

His voice rang in my ears, along with the sound of my beating heart. His grip tightened even more, and I could tell he was digging in his pocket for something. My breath became erratic, and I struggled harder against his hold. My body shook from the mix of fear and adrenaline pumping through me. I had no clue what he was digging for, but I didn't want to find out.

My struggle ceased when I heard voices growing louder from somewhere on the street. Dozens of footsteps smacked the pavement as they headed in our direction.

"Hey, who's back there?" someone yelled as they drew closer.

"Come on, hurry!" another echoed.

"Someone's in trouble. Call 911."

My heart leapt with joy at the sound of their voices and stomping feet. People were coming! They had heard my cry and were now just around the corner. *I'm saved! I'm saved!*

The man suddenly released his iron grip and slipped away from me, causing me to fall hard on my back. Not even taking a moment to focus on the pain from the impact, I quickly sat up to look around me for my attacker, but no one was there. He was gone.

I was so shaken up, I didn't have the strength to stand. I continued to cry even when the crowd of people were around me. They were all asking me a dozen questions at once while helping me get to my feet. I couldn't focus on what they were saying. I just kept looking around me, waiting for the man to come back and finish what he had started.

A man grabbed me by the shoulders and made me face him. "What happened?"

I shook my head, unable to get any words past my sobbing. My eyes darted all around us. "Did he run past you?"

"Who?" another man asked.

"Did who run past me?" the man holding my shoulders questioned.

"The man who drug me back here."

I looked to my left. The ally was a dead end with a brick wall that was at least nine feet high. He would've had to run past all of these people in order to get out of the alley. They would've seen him, or at least one of them would have. There was no way he could've gone unnoticed.

"No one came out of here. It was just you."

"No!" I said, shaking my head frantically. "That can't be!"

"Alright sweetie," a woman said as she gently patted my back. "It's okay. You're okay now. The police are on their way. They will figure this out."

As if on cue, the police car rolled up to the entrance of the alley. The red and blue lights illuminated the space in a way that allowed me to see everything. It was just an empty alleyway with a solid brick wall at the end. No doors to the buildings on either side of it, no dumpsters, nothing. No way to hide, and only one way out.

I turned back around at the sound of the car doors shutting. Two policemen walked over to where I stood.

"Alright folks. Let's clear away. Back up, back up," the officer said, waving his hands to move everyone aside. One officer followed the group of people, while the other remained with me. He turned away from the departing group and said, "I'm Officer Glenn."

I stared at his bald, fat face and said, "Raven." It came out in a raspy, hushed tone, which I hadn't intended. My nerves were still frazzled, and my heart was still racing. I couldn't stop thinking about how I'd almost died.

He pulled out a notepad and asked, "Why don't you tell me what happened?"

"Well," I started, wringing my shaking hands. I wiped at the tears on my face and took calming breaths. Meeting his eyes again, I said, "I was headed home from the bookstore when someone, a man, grabbed me and pulled me back here."

Everything replayed in my mind. His hands grabbing me, the darkness of the alley, my struggle, my cry, the roller coaster in my stomach. The world was tilting, and my fear came rushing back all at once. I could've ended up like Brendon.

He wrote my words on his notepad. Nodding, he looked back up at me. "What did your attacker look like? Try to describe him, and give me any details you can remember."

I stared at him, and my mind raced to recall what the man looked like. That's when it hit me. I never saw what he looked like. My back was to him the entire time, so I had no way of seeing him. Plus, it was so dark, and I had been terrified. The only thing that was on my mind was the need to get away. I didn't even think to look at him.

"I- I don't know. I never saw his face. He had my back against him the whole time."

"How do you know it was a man?" he asked. He waited for my response as he stared at me with beady eyes. Something behind his expression was changing. His eyes were turning less reassuring and more suspicious.

"I heard him speak. He cursed in my ear when the crowd of people came close."

He nodded and, again, jotted something down. When he finished, he tilted his head back up towards me. "How did you manage to get away?"

I shook my head and looked at all the people who had come to my rescue. They were all talking to the other officer as the police lights continued to dance off of them. "I guess when he heard people coming, he ran off."

Before Officer Glenn could respond, the other officer approached us. He was tall, and his uniform hung around his figure as if it was a tad too big for his skinny body. He had unruly brown hair with a full mustache to match.

When he stood next to Officer Glenn, he glanced at me with a skeptical gaze before saying to his partner in a not-so-subtle whisper, "No one saw the suspect leave. They said he didn't come out of the alley, and the only one they found was her."

Officer Glenn huffed and turned towards me again. He crossed his arms over his chest as he stared me down. Irritation was plastered on his face as he said, "Alright. Do you want to tell me what really happened back here?"

My mouth fell open. "I told you what happened! I was walking home when this man grabbed me and pulled me back here! I got away when all of these people scared him off!"

Tears stung my eyes again. I could feel my ears and cheeks growing hot with color. My anger was rising the more they watched me with those accusatory eyes. They were acting as though I was lying. Not only was this angering me, but I also felt fear seeping in again. What would happen if they didn't believe me?

"Miss," the other officer said. I glanced down at his name tag through hot tears. It read Blackk. I looked back up at him as he asked, "Where did your attacker go? It's a dead end." He gestured behind me as if to prove his point.

I shook my head and closed my eyes. I was shaking with

rage and nerves. They shouldn't be treating me like the suspect. I was the victim. Why couldn't they see that? Why was this so hard to believe?

"No one saw him," Glenn said. "So unless this man can fly, I don't see how he got away."

Tears rolled down my cheeks. Clenching my fists together, I said through gritted teeth, "I don't know how he got away! I'm as confused as you, but this did happen. I'm not making this up. You should be taking this more seriously, especially after what happened to Brendon."

At my outburst, the officers glanced at each other. Some sort of silent message passed between them, and they each gave a slight nod to the other. When they faced me again, Officer Glenn pursed his lips and scratched his chin. "So, Raven. Did you know Brendon?"

I blinked, wiping my tears away. "Not really."

They glanced between each other again. This time Officer Blackk addressed me. "You knew about his death. All over the news and paper. Made him pretty popular, huh?"

I slowly glanced between the two of them but didn't respond. What were they getting at exactly?

Officer Glenn sighed then pinched the bridge of his nose. "Look, if you were doing this just to get attention by being a survivor of the same attack, that isn't okay. You can get into serious trouble, and you've wasted everyone's time here."

Utterly speechless at his accusation, I had no idea how to respond. I broke down crying. I couldn't believe what was happening. They were supposed to help me, but instead, they were accusing me of lying in order to make myself famous! Frustration bubbled up in the pit of my stomach, and I so desperately wanted to go home. I couldn't do that though because I knew they would take that as a sign of guilt.

Looking them in the eyes, I pleaded, "I am not making this up, and I don't care about publicity. I was attacked, you officers came, and I was simply telling you what happened. I don't want this story going out for people to hear. In fact, I hope this incident keeps quiet. Maybe then you will see that I'm not lying."

The two officers stepped away from me to talk in hushed tones. I didn't know if they believed me, but I clearly wasn't making this up. I wouldn't be crying the way I was or pleading with them to believe me if this was some joke. I just wanted to go home and pretend that none of this had ever happened.

The officers turned back towards me. Officer Blackk pulled up his sagging pants and said, "Okay, we are going to take you down to the station where we can record your full statement. Give us any information you can on the man. Maybe an idea of how tall he was. Even that would be helpful. If this really is the same situation as Brendon's, then we need to solve this before he strikes again. Just calm down. You're safe now."

I wasn't so sure about that. I couldn't help but drag my feet as I followed them to the police car. I didn't feel safe. I felt afraid, angry, and hurt. These guys had doubted me. Even though they seemed cooperative now, that didn't mean they actually took my word on what happened. I could very well be alone in this.

But I followed along, sliding into the backseat with my heart still racing. I didn't know if it would ever slow. The adrenaline continued to pump through me, so I closed my eyes and tried to just breathe. The car lurched forward as we took off towards the police station, so my eyes turned towards the dark window as I silently prayed for this night to be over already.

***

After being at the station for three hours, recalling everything once more, attempting to give them a height, and receiving an apology from Officer Glenn and Officer Blackk, the two men drove me home. I got out of the car and slowly approached the trailer.

It was nearly 12:30, so I knew my dad would be up drinking. I didn't want the cops to see how messed up my dad was, so I lied and told them that I was going through the back door. They accepted what I said, so I went around the back of the house to wait for the sound of their squad car to drive off. When I was satisfied that they were gone, I went back around to the front door.

When I stepped inside, my dad was leaning against the kitchen counter with a half-empty bottle of vodka in one hand and a cigarette in the other. He wore the same disgusting white shirt he had been wearing for the past three days and some worn out gym shorts. His brown hair was a greasy mess that stuck up around the edges, and his once green eyes were clouded over. I shut the door as his gaze found me. He narrowed his eyes at me as he stomped towards me, sloshing alcohol in his wake.

He stood before me, swaying in a drunken state. I glanced up at him as he shouted, "Where have you been?"

His face was so close to mine that I had to hold my breath against his stench. The mix of male body odor and alcohol was not helping my already upset stomach. In reality, he probably hadn't even noticed I was gone. The only reason he did now was because he saw me come in. He rarely even remembered I existed, let alone cared whether or not I stayed out late.

"I was at the police station, Dad." I turned my head away and tried walking past him. "I was jumped and-"

He put his hand on my chest and slammed me back against the wall. I winced at the forcefulness of his shove. "At the police station? At the police station!"

He was screaming at me, and I knew he was going to turn violent at any moment. The fear from earlier was coming back all over again. I had been so afraid of the monster on the streets, that I forgot about the monster at home.

"What the hell did you do?" he yelled.

"Nothing. I was attacked on my way home. They were taking my statement. That's all."

I dared to look up at him, and he stared down at me with eyes full of rage. I gave him a pleading look, begging him to understand and believe me. The people, the police, none of them believed me. I needed someone to listen. I needed my dad to listen.

"You're a liar," he said through gritted teeth. "You are a dumb whore, Mandy!"

Tears stung my eyes. He always thought I was Mandy, my mother. He didn't ever see me as Raven. I was always Mandy.

She left us when I was a toddler. She abused drugs and slept around, which my dad found out when he came home to find her riding another man in their bedroom. Ever since then my dad has hated not only her, but me too, because he doesn't think I'm actually his. He resents me because all he can see is her. That's when everything went downhill for us, and he started his drinking.

We stood there, staring each other down for what felt like an eternity. I shook my head, preparing to walk away when he quickly slapped me across the face. The blow caused me to fall to the ground, and I cried out. I clutched my cheek as the faint taste of blood hit my tongue. My skin was throbbing and burning, the imprint of his hand forming on my face.

"Go to your room!" he screamed.

Stifling my sobs, I quickly rose to my feet and ran to my room, where I shut the door and locked it. I collapsed onto my bed and sobbed painful tears into my pillow. I could still feel his handprint stinging my skin. I didn't understand. Why did things have to be like this? Why was my life this way?

I laid there, letting all the events from the day soak in. I'd had my share of bad days, but this one had worn me down. The feeling of that man's arms gripping me tightly was still fresh in my mind, as well as the sting from the blow that my father had just dealt. Moments like this were when I found myself slipping into those endless pits of loneliness, as well as vast longing.

I longed for a real friendship and relationship that was built on love. I wanted to find the bliss that came from having someone send a sweet smile in my direction or someone who enjoyed the feeling of me in their arms. And I wanted to do the same for someone else! I was fed up with all the turmoil and hurt that came with the way things were now. Things needed to be different, and one day, I would ensure they change.

I would find that relationship. I would find the guy I was meant to be with, and I wouldn't make the same mistakes as those around me. My parents' relationship was not one I was going to go by, and neither were my failed attempts at other relationships. The time and place for finding that one special person was still unknown, but those details didn't matter to me. My heart just pleaded with God to find him soon.

Wherever he may be.

Chapter Three

S CHOOL WAS NOT MY favorite place on earth. It was rather dull and uneventful because there was no one for me to pass the time with. No friends, like normal people or boyfriends, like normal girls. No one seemed to really notice me, and I didn't beg for their attention. Being alone was kinda my thing.

Once upon a time, I did have friends. When I was in elementary school, my dad wasn't such a mess, so I spent my time playing with Barbies or playing in the mud with other kids from school. I even had a best friend who felt more like a sister than anything. Her name was Anna, and we did everything together.

That all changed though when my dad started heading off the deep end. The more he got involved with drinking and littering our home with trash, the more I noticed people distancing themselves from me. One day we were all swinging on the playground together, and the next, they ran away when I got too close. Even Anna changed. She started ignoring me and wouldn't even look in my direction anymore. As I got older, I realized their parents didn't appreciate a drunkard's daughter playing with and "influencing" their kids. I was suddenly the bad guy.

To that day, Anna and I still had classes together. Her blonde hair had gotten much longer, and her personality had become wittier and more charming. She had completely changed, both inside and out, but the only thing that hadn't changed was how she wouldn't meet my eyes. Her smile seemed to brighten a lot of people's days, but it was a smile I hadn't had turned towards me since we had stopped being sisters.

Seeing as how I was typically on my own, I made it a fun experiment to watch all the others around me. I waited for any opening to join in on a conversation or laugh about a funny memory I might have been a part of. It didn't usually happen, but I still tried.

One of the things I liked observing were people's clothing choices. The school was usually a pool of vibrant colors and patterns, so when I got to school that day, I was surprised to see the majority of the faculty and students wearing shades of gray and black in honor of Brendon's passing. "Rest In Peace" signs hung up in the hallway along with banners proclaiming that we would miss him. The mood surrounding the hallways and classroom was dreary, and a few students occasionally started crying in class. It was a very depressing Monday.

Despite the somber mood, I went through the same dragging motions of going to my classes, but when I got into

English, I actually found myself excited. We were reading one of my favorite poems, "Love's Philosophy" by Percy Bysshe Shelley. Even though I was rarely eager to be at school, this had me smiling to myself in my seat at the back of the room.

"All right," Mr. Brooks said after he finished reading the poem aloud. "I would like each of you to pair up with someone close by to discuss what you think Shelley meant with this poem."

"It's about love. Duh, Mr. Brooks," a redhead said as she popped her bubble gum.

Mr. Brooks rolled his eyes and said in a dull tone, "Thank you for that obvious statement Natalie, but remember, you all are seniors, so please, provide a more thorough answer than just *love*."

As the room erupted in chatter, I looked at the empty seat to my left. This usually happened whenever we did group work, but it never bothered me anymore. Even the teachers got used to me being partnerless because after awhile they stopped trying to pair me up with others. I had become familiar and content with this solitude.

Everyone was still busy talking when the door to the classroom opened. The room fell silent as everybody turned towards the door to see who it was.

"Sorry to interrupt," Ms. Drescle said. She was the school's nice, old office lady. Her petite body stepped into the room, and her blue rimmed glasses slid down the bridge of her nose. She pushed them back up as she said, "I have a new student with me. He is in this class."

"Ah, a new mind to mold into greatness!" Mr. Brooks

exclaimed, clapping his hands together and rubbing them as if he were trying to warm them up. "Send the child in."

Ms. Drescle stepped aside, allowing the newcomer to step into the classroom. My heart hit the floor when I saw who it was walking in. It was the guy, Landon's brother, from the day before. I still didn't know his name, but I secretly hoped that would change.

He looked just as amazing, if not more, than yesterday. He was tall and fit in all of the right places. His jet black hair was brushed to the side, falling slightly across his crystal blue eyes. He sported a fitted black t-shirt with some dark jeans, and he looked fantastic in them. He was by far the most attractive guy I had ever seen.

"What is your name, young man?" Mr. Brooks questioned once Ms. Drescle had left.

"Kaden." He gave an annoyed glance in Mr. Brooks' direction. It was one I was all too familiar with, no thanks to my awkward behavior in the store. That look only set my nerves on a frenzy even more.

"And do you have a last name?" Mr. Brooks pulled out his class role and began to write down Kaden's name. Kaden said his last name was Athelward, and Mr. Brooks nodded. "Interesting name. Well, Kaden Athelward, you may find a seat wherever you like. We are discussing a poem we just read. Whoever you partner with can fill you in."

The class went back to talking as Kaden's cool gaze scanned the room. Every girl looked at him in an adoring way, no doubt wishing he would sit with them. I secretly hoped the same, so when Kaden's eyes stopped on me, my breath caught. My cheeks grew fiery hot, and my skin blazed with an unfamiliar warmth.

I silently cursed myself for not trying to look better today. My leggings, gray sweatshirt, and ponytail weren't going to cut it. I wasn't necessarily ugly, but the way I typically dressed screamed loser and loner. What kind of person, let alone a hot guy, would want to sit next to someone like that? I'd already inwardly accepted the fact that he wasn't going to choose the seat next to mine, so when he started to make his way over to the desk by mine, my heart jumped into my throat.

He sat down with a sigh and leaned back in his chair. Glancing at him out of the corner of my eye, I gulped. He was insanely attractive. There was something almost otherworldly about him. His figure, crystal blue eyes, glossy black hair, and flawless skin looked not only handsome, but actually beautiful.

His looks didn't do much to calm my nerves, but I still dared to breathe a hesitant, "Hello."

He didn't say anything. He merely glanced at me then looked forward again.

Swallowing more of my nerves, I tried again. "I'm Raven."

"I know," he said, irritation lacing each of his words. He continued to stare forward with a smug expression. He kept his gaze focused on anything except me.

Closing my eyes, I looked away from him. I wanted to slap myself. *Of course he knows your name, idiot! You told him yesterday!*

"Um," I started, looking at him once more. "Right. Sorry. Well, do you want to discuss the poem? I can tell you what it was about since you weren't here to listen to it."

He glanced at me, a devious grin playing at his lips. "Do I *want* to discuss it?" He shook his head, laughing to himself as he faced forward again. I looked down at my feet. This was not going well. I needed to learn more social skills.

I was trying to search for something to say when he shocked me by asking, "What's the poem?" My eyes quickly darted in his direction at the sound of his voice. He was actually looking at me, which took me by surprise even more.

"It's called 'Love's Philosophy' by Per-"

"I know who it's by," he said, waving his hand dismissively. "I've read it before."

"Oh," I said. This guy, this amazingly attractive guy, had read one of my favorite poems? This was almost too good to be true. I figured based on his looks and attitude, he would be into rock or heavy metal. He didn't strike me as the type to read poetry, but maybe his behavior this far was just a facade.

He nodded before quoting, "'*What is all this sweet work worth if thou kiss not me?*'"

"Right," I smiled. The quote he chose to recite left my lips feeling naked. I felt ridiculous as a part of me wondered what it would feel like to kiss him. "Well since you've read it, we are supposed to decide what we think Percy meant with the poem."

Kaden turned to face me. He leaned in as close as our desks would allow, and his nose nearly touched mine. His warm, honey sweet breath hit my cheek as he said, "I think it's bull shit."

Taken aback by this, I pulled back away from him with a frown. "What?"

"You heard me. It's bull." He leaned back in his chair again and said, "The whole thing is him using this idea of love to get in some girl's pants. It's not about love. It's about sex. Love doesn't exist."

My jaw dropped at his words. I could feel my cheeks flushing, but it was no longer from embarrassment. This guy, whom I thought was going to be intelligent, was just pissing me off. How could he be so shallow?

"No!" I said, my anger rising. "It's about love! He is comparing different parts of nature and how they come together in love just as he wishes he and his lover could."

"Yeah. Come together as in him *in* her."

I recoiled and huffed at his remark. Through flashes of anger, I spat, "How can you be so, so-"

"Honest?" he smiled.

I wanted to slap that smile right off his face.

"Cold!" I finished. "Things like this, beautiful stories or poems, fill some of us with hope that one day we can find someone like that! Someone who will love us and care for us. Maybe even write poems like this one about us. Not all guys are perverts like you who only want sex. Guys can love someone without that."

"Is that why you're single?" he smirked.

I hesitated. "How did you know I was single?"

"Trust me. I can tell." He glanced at me from head to

toe and not in a nice way. It was more of a using my appearance to strengthen his point type of move.

"Gee, thanks." It was my turn to stare forward. I was fuming, and I didn't want to talk with him anymore. He was doing nothing except being a total jerk, so I was done wasting my time.

The rest of class felt as if it was moving in slow motion. I looked at the clock constantly, waiting for it to be time to leave, but the clock seemed to be my enemy today. The longer I sat there, listening to Mr. Brooks go on and on about true love, the more I could see Kaden staring at me through the corner of my eye.

I would glance at him every now and then. He didn't even try to hide the fact that he was staring. He had a small smile on his face, which only made me even more upset. I tried not to show my anger though because it seemed anytime I grew red from annoyance, he smiled even bigger. He thought my being mad was funny. I shook my head, furious, ready for that bell to ring.

Chapter Four

I COULDN'T STOP THINKING about Kaden at the bookstore. Some thoughts good, some thoughts bad. I had calmed down since class, which made my mind start to wonder about him. The way he smiled at me during class didn't feel malicious. Granted, it felt somewhat playful, but it didn't give me the same haughty attitude that it had at first. I wondered if maybe he wasn't actually all bad.

Perhaps teasing was his way of making friends. It was an annoying way to achieve a bond, but still, maybe he hadn't actually meant anything by it. Or maybe he was all about sex, just like he had said, and he was using his charm to try to get to me.

I hated to admit it, but it was working.

It was almost seven, which meant I would have to go soon in order to get to the Martinez house. The Martinezes' were a couple that I babysat for on Mondays so they could have a date night. Their twin daughters were six, and I was lucky that the girls usually behaved extremely well for their age. It sort of gave me a tiny break from the chaos that always surrounded me.

"Have a wonderful night," I said as the last woman walked out of the door.

She threw a hand up to signal a goodbye as she left. I did my routine for closing up, making sure everything was secure in its place. I walked over to the door and flipped the sign to close, but didn't lock the door yet since I still had to leave through it. I turned to head back to the counter, but the sound of the glass door opening made me stop in my tracks. I spun around, only to come face to face with someone I never would've expected.

"Kaden?" I asked, stepping back slightly. "What are you doing here? Can you not read? The sign clearly says closed." I pointed at the sign just to prove my point.

He was grinning from ear to ear. He shoved his hands in his jeans pockets as he leaned back against the wall. Some of his hair fell down in his face, but he quickly ran a hand through it, putting the strands back in place. Despite my mixed feelings about him, my heart jumped a little at the contrast of his dark hair against those beautiful blue eyes.

"I can read. I just chose to ignore it."

I rolled my eyes and walked behind the counter. He followed and leaned across it, still smiling at me. He was too close to me, so I placed my hand on his chest to push him back slightly. That only amused him more. Laughing, he turned in a circle to look around the room. "So, you work in a bookstore."

"Clearly," I said, waving my hand around the room.

He looked at me again. He was smiling and shaking his head. "What a loser."

I pulled my hands into fists and shook with anger. "You know what, if you're just going to be a jerk then I don't know why you bothered coming here!"

He chuckled slightly and walked closer to me, closing the distance between us. He poked my shoulder and said, "Because messing with you is funny as hell. You should see your face when you get mad. You look like a gothic Tinker Bell."

I stepped back, trying to catch my breath again. He was so close that I had forgotten to breathe. I had to remember I was angry at him. He could not make me forget that just by looking at me with those amazing blue eyes or by standing too close.

Well, maybe he could make me forget. That's why I stepped back. I couldn't let him get me sidetracked.

"Gee, thanks," I mumbled as I grabbed my bag and the keys.

"Where are you going now?" he asked as he followed me out the door.

I locked the store and put the keys in my bag. It was getting darker outside, which made my skin crawl. Looking down the sidewalk, my eyes drifted to the alley where I was attacked. I gulped and looked at Kaden, realizing he'd just asked me a question. "I'm going to babysit now."

"Oh. So let me get this straight. You're a loser with no friends or boyfriend, you're a hopeless romantic, you're a nerd who likes books, and you're a goody-two-shoes babysitter. Wow. The stuff you learn about someone in a day."

He flashed one of his smiles again, making my heart flutter. But I ignored that feeling. I pressed it down and let all my anger boil up until I felt like I was going to explode. Still, I chose not to say anything. Instead, I just turned away from him and walked towards the Martinez house. I wasn't going to fight this battle. I was good at turning the other cheek in order to be the bigger person.

As I walked away from him, the sound of footsteps following close behind me rang in my ears, and I could practically feel his eyes boring into the back of my head. I sighed in irritation, and he laughed behind me.

"Are you mad, Tinker Bell?"

I spun around and narrowed my eyes at him. "Why are you following me?"

He shrugged and said, "I just felt like walking you to wherever it is we're going."

My stomach did a backflip. He wanted to walk me to the Martinezes'? I looked away, knowing that I was blushing. Having a guy walk me to work or home had always been a sort of fantasy for me. The fact that Kaden was doing this was enough to make me blush, even if he wasn't the kind of guy I had pictured to do it.

I caught my breath then looked back at him. "Fine. Since you are new in town and don't seem to have any other people to bug, you can walk with me. But can you not make such mean comments if you are going to be staying with me all the way there?"

He smiled again. "Whatever you want."

We started walking again, side by side this time. My heart was beating a mile a minute from him being so close to me, but when I saw an alley coming up, I stopped dead in my tracks. My eyes bore into its dark entryway, and my anxiety raced through my body. Every inch of me tingled with a rush of fear. This alley was near the edge of town, so there was hardly anyone around. I was petrified of the thought of someone hiding in there, waiting to snatch me again.

Kaden looked back at me, confused as to why I'd stopped. His smile slowly disappeared as he followed my line of sight and realization crossed his face. He walked over to me, and to my surprise, he slipped his arm around my waist, pulling me closer to his side. Looking at me out of the corner of his eye, he smiled once more. This smile was different than all the others he had worn so far. This one met his eyes despite its small, gentle curl at the sides.

His rich voice softly wrapped around me as he said, "Trust me. Nothing is going to get you while I'm here."

My cheeks grew warm, and my knees became weak. He was holding me! One minute he was spouting out asshole comments and the next, he acted as if we had been extremely close this entire time. I considered the possibility that maybe his being a jerk was him flirting. I wished he was flirting, but did that mean he only wanted sex out of me? He'd said so himself - he only cared about sex from a girl.

We drew closer to the alley. My heart drummed against my chest with every step we took. I braced myself for something to happen as we walked past it. I refused to look inside, fearing I would see a man dressed all in black, holding a knife or gun, ready to kill me. But there was nothing. Nothing happened. We had made it past, safe and sound.

Once we were a few feet away from it, Kaden let his arm fall from around me. He moved away from me slightly so he could smile down at me. "See. You're safe with me."

His words and smile made me blush even more. And what was that look he kept giving me? Playfulness? A friendly smile? Longing? I wish I knew.

"Thanks," I said, and I actually meant it. It was a lot easier to walk past that alley with someone next to me.

I started walking again as I attempted to clear my head from the remaining mixture of nerves and anxiety. We ran across the street onto another sidewalk that went along the entrances to different streets with houses on them. We were getting close to the Martinezes'.

He looked down at me. "Does that Brendon guy's murder have you freaked out about alleys?"

I was feeling so many emotions right then, but I swallowed them down and answered, "Last night, on my way home from the bookstore, I was jumped. Someone dragged me into an alley." I closed my eyes, reliving the moment. The experience was still so fresh that my eyes teared up at the memory. "I don't know what would've happened if people hadn't shown up."

I glanced at him. He was no longer smiling, and he had a far off look on his face. He ducked his head and kicked a rock. "That sounds awful."

I wiped a tear that was trying to escape and laughed at his bluntness. "Tell me about it. But I'm here. That's all that matters. It will just take some time for me to get comfortable walking past alleys again."

We walked the rest of the way in silence. I wanted to talk more because I was actually enjoying talking to him now that he wasn't being a jerk, but he still had that distant look. It felt good to open up about what happened after no one else would listen or believe me. A weight was lifted off of me, but I wasn't going to press the subject anymore. I decided to leave him be until we arrived at the Martinezes'. Climbing the stairs of the porch, I turned to look at him.

"Well," I started, "I'm here. Thanks for walking me."

He didn't say anything. He just looked at me for a long time. Those blue eyes stared into mine with some hidden thought, and I stared back at him as I tried to piece together what that look could mean.

Just when I thought he was going to say something, he turned and left. He didn't give any warning. He just spun around and walked away without saying goodbye or anything. I stood there, feeling somewhat disappointed at his abrupt departure. My eyes followed him, his silhouette getting smaller the further he walked away.

***

I flopped down on the couch inside the Martinezes' two story home. Lounging back on the plush cushions felt like heaven. I had just finished washing up the dishes from dinner and putting the kids to bed. There was still an hour before the

Martinezes' were supposed to come home from their date night, so I decided to relax by watching some TV.

I was lying back against the couch, yawning, when the lights and TV flicked off. Startled by the sudden darkness, I sat up, and it took a few moments for my heart to stop racing. After a moment of letting my mind catch up with what had happened, I pieced together that the power had gone off. I slowly stood and peeked out the window. All the other houses lining the street still had power, and it wasn't storming. I didn't understand why the house had suddenly lost power.

I let out a nervous breath and mumbled to myself, "Don't ask questions. You're just going to freak yourself out."

I walked into the kitchen and got a flashlight out of the junk drawer. If it wasn't the weather then it must be the breaker, so I would have to go into the basement to check it. My stomach twisted, and my hands grew clammy at the thought of going into the dark basement on my own. I wasn't a little kid, but that didn't mean I wasn't allowed to be afraid.

I tried swallowing away my nerves as I opened the basement door. The old door creaked on its hinges as a gust of cold air hit me. I shivered and took another attempt at a calming breath. The smell of mildew swarmed around me as I made my descent down into the dark room.

When I reached the bottom, it was pitch black. I pressed the button on the side of the flashlight, but nothing happened. My skin crawled, and my heart stopped. I smacked the cold metal against my hand, but it still didn't come on. I groaned and stomped my foot in frustration. I guessed I would have to go find a different flashlight back upstairs.

I turned and grabbed the hand railing to make my way back up when hands went around my waist. My stomach leapt into my throat as I was jerked backwards. The strong tug caused me to fall hard on my back against the concrete floor. It knocked the breath out of me, preventing me from screaming, and an awful ring filled my ears.

Before I could think about what just happened, a heavy body straddled me, and the attacker placed their hands on my neck. I grabbed at their wrists as they started to squeeze, preventing me from screaming or breathing. My heart was racing as pressure built up in my head. I tried to dig my nails into the hands, but they were not letting up. Tears poured down my cheeks as I squirmed underneath them, terrified for my life. It was getting so hard to breathe. I needed air.

I needed it now.

As the pressure on my neck became even harder, gurgling sounds escaped my lips, and I kept opening and closing my mouth in a futile attempt to reach for any air I could. I lost a grip on their hands because fuzziness was taking over my head. My hands slipped away from the grip holding me. I didn't have enough strength to reach back up and fight.

I was going to die.

Just when I thought I was going to be done for, the hands strangling me loosened their hold and then dropped away all together. I sucked air back into my lungs and choked as I took deep, thankful breaths. I clutched at my neck, trying to make the awful burn in my throat stop.

The attacker stood as I laid on the floor, still too weak to do anything except suck in large gulps of air. Their footsteps headed in the direction of the door at the far end of the basement that led to the outside. The Martinezes' never locked that door, and I knew right then that was how this person had gotten in.

I tilted my head back slowly, trying to get a glimpse of whoever it was as they left. I prayed that there would be enough light outside to get some sort of idea of who they were or what they looked like. I couldn't go to the cops blindly again, so I watched as the door opened.

It was so dark out that I wasn't able to see anything important about them. I could see they had the build and broad body structure of a guy though, and he was dressed in black. He turned away from the door and disappeared from my sight. I sighed, happy to feel air moving through my body again. My head was still spinning, and dark spots clouded my vision. I took another deep breath before letting the hungry hands of darkness consume me.

Chapter Five

I WOKE UP TO hands gently shaking me. When I opened my eyes, the lights were back on, and Mrs. Martinez was leaning over me with worry written on her beautiful caramel colored face. Her glossy, dark hair framed her petite features, and her chocolate colored eyes scanned every inch of me.

"Oh Raven, sweetie! Are you okay?" she cried.

I slowly reached my shaking hand up to my head. It was throbbing like crazy. She helped me to sit up, gently guiding my back as I went. I took slow breaths as I answered, "Yeah. I think I'm okay."

Mr. Martinez, who had been fixing the breaker, walked over to us. He still wore his button up shirt and black trousers from their date, and his chestnut colored hair was still perfectly styled. He squatted down and asked, "What happened?"

I glanced between each of them as I debated what to say. I didn't have any proof that someone had attacked me again. There was nothing around us when he was choking me, so there was no sign of a struggle. Not only that, I still didn't have anything to identify him by.

I'm sure they would have believed me if I told them what happened, but they would insist on calling the cops. I knew the cops wouldn't believe me after last night though. Plus, it is pretty hard to believe that someone would break into the house, try to kill me, then stop for no reason whatsoever. I still didn't understand that part myself.

"Um," I started. "The power went off, so I came down here to check the breaker. I fell coming down the steps because it was dark. I guess when I fell it knocked me out." I reached up, rubbing my head again.

"You need to be more careful, honey," Mrs. Martinez said.

She and her husband helped me get to my feet. My legs felt like jello. I thought I was going to fall back down, but they helped to steady me. With each of them aiding me, we walked up the stairs and into the kitchen. Mrs. Martinez had me sit down and drink a glass of water while Mr. Martinez went upstairs to check on the girls.

"I'm so sorry you got hurt," Mrs. Martinez said as she sat down next to me. She was looking at me when she got a perplexed look on her face. "Raven, what happened to your neck?"

"My neck?" I asked, reaching up to touch it. Pain flared up beneath my touch, so I knew my neck was bruised. Instantly, I hesitated. My mind raced as I tried to decide what to do. Bruises meant proof, and proof was good. Was it enough though?

After my first go around with the Officers, I felt reluctant anytime I thought about seeking their help. The fear of them questioning or suspecting me for foul play was still at the forefront of my head. I wasn't ready to seek out their help just yet, which meant I couldn't let Mrs. Martinez know the truth either. She'd definitely suggest we seek their help.

I swallowed and shook my head at her. I had to come up with an excuse so as not to worry her more. I had to keep the truth hidden, at least for now.

I gave a dismissive smile. "Oh that! It's nothing. I just had an accident the other day."

I knew that was vague, which meant she probably wasn't going to buy it, so I was surprised and thankful when she didn't push me any further. That was something I always appreciated about the Martinezes'. They knew my situation, and they also knew I didn't like to talk about it. This meant they never tried to push me for answers. If I wanted to tell them, I would.

Mr. Martinez came back downstairs and approached the table. He sat down next to his wife and gently placed a loving hand on her back. He nodded to her as he said, "The girls are sound asleep." When his eyes found mine, he asked, "Do you need a ride home, Raven?"

He offered to take me home every time I babysat, and each time, I declined. I didn't like people knowing what kind of a dump I lived in, even if it wasn't by choice. Even so, the Martinezes' knew what kind of home life I had. They were some of the few people in town who didn't look down on me for it.

Despite never accepting Mr. Martinez's offer, tonight I was feeling more inclined to let him drive me home. Sure I preferred walking, but with the two near death experiences I'd had, I didn't want to walk home alone in the dark. It terrified me to think about what could happen when I left their house. Whoever had been attacking me could be waiting for exactly that.

I smiled and said, "If you don't mind. Falling down the stairs has me a bit shaken up."

He nodded and attempted to give me a reassuring smile. "I understand."

He stood and kissed his wife on top of the head. Their affection for each other always made me smile, and I hoped that someone would love me one day the way Mr. Martinez loved his wife.

I told Mrs. Martinez goodnight, and she gave me my pay, as well as one last worried glance. I tried to politely ignore her look as I followed Mr. Martinez out into the night. A chill ran through me as we stepped out onto the dark porch. I swallowed hard, looking around for any sign of someone standing in the shadows, waiting for the moment when they could attack.

"Raven, are you coming?"

The sound of Mr. Martinez's voice pulled me back to reality, and I realized he was already standing by the car. I had been so busy looking around, I didn't realize that he had already walked to the car. Standing alone on the dark porch sent a chill down my arms, so I dashed to the passenger side. I climbed in with an apologetic smile, and I let the relief of being inside the car wash over me.

The drive home was fine. We mainly just made small talk. He asked me about school, and I asked him about work. It was just an easy way of keeping my mind distracted from everything that had gone on. I didn't want to dwell on the fact that I had been attacked again, making that twice within two days.

We finally pulled up to my trailer, and Mr. Martinez let me out. He glanced at the disaster of a structure with a hint of disgust on his face. It looked filthy, but he knew it wasn't me. It was all my dad.

Mr. Martinez turned back to me as I got out and said, "Thanks again, Raven. Be careful, all right?"

I smiled and said, "Yes sir."

I shut the car door and approached the trailer as the car lights left me. I slowly crept inside. The lights were off except for the TV and the light above the sink. My dad was leaning against the counter in the kitchen, mumbling to himself about my mom leaving him. I was happy to see he finally changed into some clean clothes. Although the tilted angle he held his beer at told me he probably wasn't going to stay clean much longer.

My heart broke slightly for him because I knew he really missed my mom. He had let his life get away from him because of it, but I couldn't comfort him. He never wanted anything to do with me.

I crept past the living room and slinked down the

hallway to my room. Quietly shutting the door, I sighed in relief. I slumped against the wooden frame and reached my hands up to brush them softly against my neck. It hurt when I barely even touched it. Whomever had done this had a very strong grip.

I walked over to my bedside table to turn my lamp on before walking to the mirror to look at the damage. Dark purple marks were already forming around the center of my neck, where the monster's hands had been. I could still feel his grip on my neck, trying to squeeze every last breath out of me.

Why stop, though? Why would he stop when that could give me a chance to report him and get him caught? Granted, I didn't go to the police, but he had no way of knowing that I wouldn't. So why just stop? I think that was one of the most horrifying parts about all of this. The suspense of his possible motivation and the fear of what he might do next.

***

I slumped down in my desk and pulled my scarf more firmly around my neck. I made it through the whole day without any questions or suspicious looks, so now I just had to make it through English. I wore a scarf to hide the bruises that were still very much visible, but part of me regretted it. The skin was even more sensitive to the touch now, and the scarf didn't help with that. I just didn't want anyone to see the marks, so I sucked it up and pushed through the pain.

When Kaden walked in, I stopped fiddling with the scarf and watched as he approached the seat next to mine.

He had a sullen look on his face as he walked with his eyes toward the ground, and when he finally looked at me, his frown deepened.

"Hey," I smiled.

He slowly dropped down into his seat and leaned across the aisle. His heavy gaze bore into mine with concern etched into his face. His eyes traveled from mine to glide down my face before stopping at my neck. Thinking he saw the markings, I swallowed hard. I tried pulling the scarf up more, hoping that none of the bruises were showing, but he reached out and carefully grabbed my hand.

I stopped breathing momentarily at the feel of his soft hand holding mine. His touch was gentle and soothing. It felt so familiar and safe. He lowered my hand back to my lap and carefully pulled the scarf away from my neck to reveal the hidden marks. I closed my eyes and turned away from him as I grew nervous. This attention was the exact opposite of what I wanted, and he was the last person I wanted to see me like this.

"What happened?" he asked, his voice catching a little.

"Nothing," I said. I worked to fix my scarf in order to hide the bruising. I should've fixed it better before he came in the classroom, because obviously I hadn't covered the spots all the way.

"That doesn't look like nothing," he said. His tone sounded almost angry.

I looked at him, and he had a scowl on his face. His eyes turned dark, and his jaw clenched. He was acting so different. He made it seem as if he cared, which was strange for him since he had been mostly nothing but a jerk since I met him.

I shook my head in frustration. "I just had a little accident. That's all."

He rolled his eyes. "What kind of accident?"

I bit my lip and stared at him. His concerned eyes were searching me in such a way that my walls started breaking down. I reluctantly decided to be honest with him. "I was attacked again last night. Not in an alley, but actually at the Martinezes' house."

I stopped there. I didn't feel the need to elaborate, nor did I want to recall the memory. I closed my eyes and absently rubbed at my neck. My throat was getting tight from emotion once more.

He reached over to me, and my eyes shot open as he gently pulled my fingers away from my neck. He stared at my hand, rubbing the top of it softly. A warm pulse spread underneath his touch, and it slowly moved throughout my body. I swallowed hard, not knowing what else to do. Where had this affection come from all of a sudden?

Seeing the way he tenderly touched my hand sent flutters through my stomach. This felt so familiar, but I had no idea why. No one had ever touched me like this, but for some reason he sent a pulse of adoration and a sense of familiarity through me.

Finally, he looked at me with those dazzling blue eyes. They stared into mine with an unfamiliar heat; however, the more I looked at his eyes, the more I felt like I had seen them somewhere before. There was no way though. I had never seen eyes like his. Well, except for the day when-

"Are you okay?" he asked, cutting off my thoughts.

I didn't trust my voice, so I nodded. He looked back to my hand again and swallowed. He seemed so different today. I couldn't take my eyes off his perfect figure, sitting next to me as he caressed my hand. My breath was stuck in my throat, and my mind raced to figure out all of the emotions coursing through me.

Neither of us said anything after that. Class started, so he let go of my hand to face the front. I followed suit, folding my hands in my lap. I looked down at them as my heart continued to pound. His touch had been so warm and soothing. I didn't want to let go.

Chapter Six

THE NEXT DAYS AND even weeks were a lot more peaceful. I was able to go to work and school without any more attacks. The news was also clear of any other murders. I was thankful that things seemed to be returning to normal.

The memories were still there for me, but Kaden made dealing with them a lot easier. Over the next two months, I found myself growing much closer to him. We usually ate lunch together during school, and sometimes he would pop into the bookstore just to say hi to me.

On one occasion, it was slower than usual at the bookstore, so Mrs. Morea had me rearranging the bookcases and displays. I was just debating whether to use the black or white display when Kaden walked in. A smile lit up my face when I saw him. He was dressed in a fitted white t-shirt paired with dark jeans. The contrast of such a light colored shirt with his dark hair had my cheeks flushing slightly.

I never stopped finding him attractive.

"Hey," I said with a smile. I stopped digging around in the supply box to stand up straight. I walked closer to him as he came further into the store.

Grinning, he waved a hand at me. His other remained casually behind his back as he glanced around the store. "Busy?"

Books and decorations were lying all about as I worked to sort through everything. There was still space to walk, but boxes lined the majority of the room. It looked a bit chaotic, which was why I usually used slow days to do this.

I laughed and looked around at the mess. "It's cluttered, I know. I'm rearranging our displays and decorations. Mrs. Morea had a fit today, complaining that we needed a change of scenery, so here we are."

"Interesting," he mumbled as he spun one of the rotating bookmark displays.

My eyes traveled down his arm to where it disappeared behind his back. He glanced up at me and grinned. He looked briefly over his shoulder at what he was hiding, then his blue eyes found their way back to mine. Bringing his arm out from behind his back, I held my breath as my eyes fell upon the deep, rich red petals.

He smiled sheepishly as he held a single rose out to me. "It's for you."

My heart pounded as giddiness flooded through me. My smile went from ear to ear as I gently took the flower from his fingers. I held the stem as I brought it up to my nose. I inhaled, and the sweet scent filled my head, making me dizzy with delight.

Nervous and red from my emotions, I continued to stare down at the lush petals as I asked, "What made you get me a rose?"

"I passed a flower shop on the way into town, and they had a sign out front that said they'd just gotten in some fresh roses. I guess when I read it, I thought that you might like one, so I got it for you."

The color in my cheeks deepened, and my heart fluttered. I didn't think I was going to be able to hold in the bliss that was on the verge of seeping out of me.

"Do you like it?" he asked, grinning at me with a gleam in his eye.

Finding the courage to look up at him, I nodded. "I love it. Thank you." I breathed in its sweet aroma again and observed the velvety soft petals. "It really is beautiful."

He nodded. "I think that's why I liked it so much. It's beauty reminded me of yours."

I blushed and quickly averted my eyes to look at my feet. A wave of heat flooded the inside of my chest as I repeated his words over and over in my head. This was the first time he'd said something like that in the months we had spent together. It made my heart swell with delight.

He chuckled at my embarrassment and headed towards the exit. "Well," he started. He turned to look back at me as he reached the door. "I have to head out. I just wanted to stop by to give that to you."

I nodded at him, still unable to look directly at him. Taking calming breaths, I said, "All right. Thank you again for the rose."

His face remained lit up as he gave me one final look, and his wide grin reached his bright eyes, which made them crinkle at the sides. "Of course."

My eyes followed him as he left the store and joined the people on the sidewalks. I watched him as long as the windows of the store made it possible, and only after he was out of view did I release the breath I had been holding.

That day, that moment, stuck with me, even after the month came to an end. He continued making visits to see me at work, and I found our relationship deepening. We were friends, but our interactions at school and his visits to the store sent a surge of happiness through me that I wasn't used to feeling.

He still made little jokes at me every now and then, but they were no longer offensive. I always found myself laughing along with him or making jokes right back at him. I had never laughed with anyone the way I did with him. He brought out a side of me that I never even knew I had, and I had to admit that I loved the way it felt.

I loved the way I could laugh and just be myself with him. I never had to think about the loneliness I felt at home because he left no room for that. If I wasn't smiling, he did whatever was necessary to bring that smile to my lips.

We had yet to hang out outside of school, besides his occasional visits to my work, so I was both surprised and elated when he arrived to class one day and asked, "Do you maybe want to go out to dinner tonight?"

My chin dropped slightly. Excitement flared up inside of me. He stared at me with a slight grin playing at his lips, no doubt finding my loss of words amusing.

Tonight was one of my few breaks from work, so I was completely free. I couldn't help but grin at him as I answered, "Sure."

He smiled even bigger at me and leaned back in his seat. "Where do you want to go?"

I shrugged and said, "It doesn't matter to me. I'm shocked that you asked. It was very-" I paused, "unexpected. In a good way though."

"Well, I'm full of surprises." He gave me another mischievous grin.

I laughed slightly. Of course, I'd thought about going out to do something together, especially as we seemed to be growing closer. I never did suggest anything, though because Kaden always seemed content with just seeing each other at school and at the bookstore. I didn't want to allow myself to get the wrong idea and push things further than what he actually intended. I was still somewhat afraid that I was the only one developing these strong emotions.

We spent the rest of the class focused on the lesson. Well, more or less. I couldn't settle down. I was so excited that Kaden wanted to take me out. I didn't know what made him decide to finally ask, but I wasn't complaining. All I wanted was to go out and have a good night with him. I had never been on a date, so my mind raced all during class as I tried to figure out what I was supposed to do and say.

I looked at him sideways. He was facing forward, not focused on anything. His gaze was wandering off into space, and his brow was furrowed in deep thought. I wondered what he was dwelling on and what he was so perplexed by. He seemed bothered or confused about something.

I faced forward again. My stomach twisted slightly as I started telling myself he regretted asking me out. This led to a stream of thoughts in my head, like what if he was troubled because he didn't actually like me. After spending these past few months together, I really thought that something was growing between us, but maybe that was just wishful thinking. He could've been using me as an easy way to get some.

I closed my eyes, swallowing away the sickening feeling rising in my stomach. I didn't want to believe that he was in this for sex. If he was and he tried to pull something tonight, he was going to be in for a rude awakening. He wouldn't be getting anything from me, and if he pushed me away after that then I would know that it wasn't real after all. But that would be determined after tonight, so I forced a smile onto my lips and focused on what I hoped would be a wonderful night to come.

The bell rang, signifying the end of the school day. The room erupted in sound as everyone gathered their belongings to head home. I stood to pack my bag when I felt Kaden's arm slip around my waist.

Blushing, I looked up at him as he smiled and asked, "Mind if I walk you home?"

I shook my head as I grew flustered. All of my worries and doubts vanished instantly at his warm touch. I could barely contain myself as we walked out of the classroom together, and my head spun as different emotions raced through me. My heart was pounding so hard that I was sure he could hear it, but he just kept smiling and walking, with his arm draped around me.

This caused a slew of girls to stare at us, adoring him and sneering at me. I'd figured I just made a lot of their hate lists, but I raised my head higher and smiled. His arm was around me, not them.

When we made it outside, I looked up at him and smiled. "What brought all of this on?"

"What do you mean?" he asked.

His blue eyes gazed down at me, and a wave of uncertainty quickly clouded his face. I swore I saw regret in his eyes, but the look was gone so quickly that I couldn't be sure. I swallowed. What did he regret? I was beginning to fear that he really did regret acting this way towards me, and a part of me prayed that wasn't the case.

"I don't know." I looked down at my feet and kicked a rock.

He didn't say anything. He just stared forward at the tree line and road that lead towards my house. I couldn't tell if he was angry or just thinking. His face was an expressionless mask. Maybe he didn't like talking about his feelings, unlike me. I mean, I wore my heart on my sleeve. He could just be the complete opposite when it came to certain topics.

Not wanting to make things any more awkward than I already had, I said, "Nevermind. I'm happy that you asked. It's nice being able to actually go out together."

His smile was back in an instant as he looked at me.

That warm gleam returned to his eyes as he said, "Well, I'm glad you said yes. That would've been embarrassing if you'd said no. You would've killed my pride." He put his hand on his chest and faked heart ache.

I laughed and said, "Oh, well we wouldn't want that now would we?"

He smiled even broader at me, making his blue eyes crinkle at the sides. His smile sent butterflies through my stomach and made my knees grow weak. I looked away quickly, feeling my cheeks growing too warm for comfort. I could hear him laughing softly at my reaction to his smile, which only made me grow more red. I wrung my hands nervously as I attempted to change the subject.

"So, where do you want to go tonight?"

He shrugged and said, "I'm still pretty new here, remember? I don't know any good places."

"Oh, right."

Color warmed my cheeks yet again. At least that was something I was good at - making a fool of myself and blushing about it. I sighed at the uncertainty of our plans until an idea occurred to me. Perking up, I asked, "Well, do you maybe want to do something before dinner? Are you doing anything right now?"

He looked at me with a curious raised brow. "Why? What do you have in mind?"

I smiled and grabbed his hand, running in the direction of my house. I could hear him panting and laughing, asking where we were going, but I wouldn't say. It was a surprise! I pushed further along the stretch of road when I realized my mistake. I couldn't let him see the dump I lived in.

I abruptly stopped running, causing him to run right into the back of me. He hit me with such force that we both went tumbling to the ground. I braced myself for the impact of the fall, but before I collided with the ground, he grabbed my waist, pulling my back to his chest. He turned our bodies as we fell the rest of the way, causing me to land on top of him. He grunted as he hit the ground, and I quickly jumped to my feet.

"Oh my gosh!" I squealed. "Are you okay?" I slowly reached out, taking his arm to help him to his feet.

He laughed as we brushed the dirt off the back of his shirt. "I'm fine. It didn't hurt. I'm just glad you're okay." He looked at me then, forcing a smile as concern etched into the corners of his eyes. I stared at him as he continued. "Why did you stop running like that? What happened?"

"Oh, that," I said, looking away in embarrassment. "I just wanted you to wait here while I went inside my house for a minute."

He looked around at the vacant road and woods behind him. He crossed his arms and said, "You want me to wait here?" He looked back at me and said, "Wouldn't it make more sense for me to actually wait outside your house, or maybe even inside?" He raised his eyebrow at me.

I shook my head and said, "I mean probably, but my house isn't all that great." I looked away and tugged on a strand of my hair in frustration. Looking back at him, I said, "Please. Just wait here. I don't want you to see my house. It's-" I hesitated, "a real dump. I don't want you to think that's the kind of person I am."

He smiled again. This one displayed a kind warmth instead of his usual sexy charm. My heart fluttered. I liked this smile even more than the one he pulled for appeal. He stepped closer to me and said, "I don't care where you live. So what? You may live in a dump, but that doesn't bother me. I won't judge. I promise."

I squinted my eyes and slightly tilted my head at him as I tried to decide what to do. It was so easy to trust him and let him see all the parts of me, even the bad ones. His unwavering gaze and smile eased its way through my wavering heart. Finally, I sighed and relented.

Pointing my finger at him, I said, "Fine. You can wait outside my house, but if you say one thing about it, I'm never bringing you back here again!"

He smiled even broader and took my hand in his. I matched his expression, and we turned to walk towards my trailer. Nerves crashed through me as I pictured all of the different possible reactions he could have. I didn't have much time to think about it though. When we reached it, we stopped walking. I nervously looked at him to gauge his reaction, but he was still just smiling at me. Relief flooded me, and it felt easier to breathe when I knew for sure he wasn't judging me.

Letting go of his hand, I said, "Okay, you wait here. I'm just going to change and then we can go."

"Go where? You still haven't told me where we are going."

"You'll see," I said as I darted inside.

My dad was sitting in his recliner watching an unfamiliar movie as I slipped into my room. I took my hair down from the ponytail it was in, letting my black curls slip down my back. My heart was pounding as I tried to decide what to wear. Tonight was obviously something special since I was finally going out with Kaden, so I wanted to do more than my usual leggings and a shirt.

Nodding, I tugged a deep purple dress from the closet. The soft fabric stopped just above my knees, and it hugged my upper body while falling loose past my waist. I paired it with some black laced fishnet tights and black ankle boots. After applying just a bit of mascara and blush, I turned towards my full-body mirror.

Looking at my reflection, I smiled and decided I looked nice. The bruises that had been on my neck from that night at the Martinezes' were basically gone by now. There was still a slight discoloration on my neck where the marks had been, but to anyone else, it probably just looked like an odd shadow. I did a final once-over then nodded at my reflection. I excitedly left my room to go outside and meet Kaden.

"Okay, I'm ready" I said.

He was staring into the woods when I came out. When he heard me, he turned in my direction. As soon as his gaze fell on me, he froze. He looked at me from head to toe, then back again, with his mouth hanging slightly open. It made my knees grow weak, and my stomach did a somersault. His gaze always seemed to do that to me. I stared at him and smiled.

"You look," Kaden started before pausing to look me

over once more. When his eyes found mine again, he smiled and finished, "Stunning."

"Thanks," I blushed.

He came closer to me, looking at me with a mesmerized expression. When he finally reached me, his eyes scanned my features. They traced every part of my face and slowly moved down my neck. That's when he grew stiff. He cleared his throat and glanced away. He had just noticed the faded marks on my neck.

Anytime Kaden noticed the marks, he always turned somber. They seemed to really bother him, which in a weird way made me feel somewhat special. It felt nice to be worried about, although I hated that he felt legitimately bothered by it. Especially now when they were barely even visible.

He shook his head before turning back to meet my eyes. Shoving his hands in his pockets, he asked, "So, what do you want to do right now?"

Excitedly, I took his hand and headed into the woods next to my house. "I want to take you to a place that I always went to when I was growing up. It's beautiful! You'll love it."

We walked deeper into the woods, the trees creating a darkness resembling twilight. We continued to walk down a slope, climbing over fallen trees and ducking under hanging limbs. I felt my stomach leap when we finally broke through the trees to the place I had missed for two long years.

My clearing, full of a beautiful, gold light, was finally before me. It was just as I remembered. The water was still crystal clear, with the bed of vibrant green clovers next to it. The trees surrounding it created a perfect circle, allowing sunlight to bathe the area in the most beautiful light.

A warm smile lit my face as I glanced at Kaden. He was gazing around at everything before him in utter amazement. His blue eyes were wide as he took in every detail, tracing our surroundings carefully. I felt a swarm of happiness flow through me as his eyes traveled around my clearing. I looked back around it as well.

I didn't know what had made me want to bring Kaden here. I had never shown this place to anyone because it was sacred and mine, but something inside of me made me want to share it with him. I wanted to welcome him into my safe haven just as I had welcomed him into the rest of my life.

I turned to look back at him, but as soon as I did, my smile fell. His previously amazed expression had changed. He now wore such a pained mask on his face as he looked around. The corners of his mouth were turned down, and his brow was creased in a way that made it look like he had just received a physical blow to the chest. My eyes narrowed in worry and confusion. I looked back around the clearing to see what could be causing this sort of reaction from him, but I couldn't find anything wrong.

I took a step to stand in front of him, peering up into his distressed blue eyes. "What's wrong?"

He looked at me, staring into my eyes for what felt like an eternity. A smile slowly spread across his features, and the pained expression faded away. He gently shook his head as he said, "Nothing. It's nothing. It's really incredible here."

He looked back to the clearing, his eyes tracing over every inch of it. He took my hand, and as if he knew where to go, he led me to the clover patch, where we sat down together by the water.

He leaned back on his hands as he turned towards me. "How did you find this place?"

I shrugged and said, "I don't know. One day when I was little, I wanted to escape my life at home. I ran into the woods to hide, and I just kept running until I found this place. After that, I would just always come here when I needed to get away. It was so calm and peaceful." I smiled before adding, "It was my paradise."

"Was? As in past tense? You don't come here anymore?" I looked at him and shook my head. He stared at me and swallowed hard. He paused for a brief moment before asking, "What made you stop coming?"

I turned away from him to look at the pond. I needed time to gather my answer to that question, so I slowly reached my finger in to twirl it around in the cool water. "I don't know. I used to think that when I came here there was someone always close by. Someone watching over me. Once I even thought I saw a glimpse of them in the water, but the next time I came here that feeling was gone. I didn't feel as comforted here anymore."

I swallowed hard as the memory came back to me. I'd been so disappointed and hurt that day, when I'd come to find a clearing that no longer felt like home. Shaking my head, I tossed away the painful memory and returned to the moment before me.

I felt ridiculously dumb for just spilling all of that out to him. I decided not to mention the experience with the wolf though, because there was no way he would believe that. I wasn't sure if I even believed it myself, and *I* was there.

I looked over at him to find him staring at me. I cringed and said, "I probably sound crazy, huh?"

He shook his head while looking at me with sad eyes. "No."

We stared into each other's eyes for what felt like forever. The more he looked at me, the sadder his eyes became. It was killing me seeing him so distraught, but I didn't understand what was making him so sad.

Finally, I couldn't take that look anymore. It was twisting my stomach in a painful way, so before I knew what I was doing, I leaned over and kissed him softly on his cheek. My body froze as my mind caught up to what I'd just done. Swallowing my nerves, I glanced up at him sheepishly.

I knew that every inch of me was glowing red, but I didn't care. I just wanted to comfort him, to ease the sorrow etched on his face, but he didn't return any sort of affection. He just turned away from me, now wearing a conflicted mask, and he ran a hand through his hair.

My skin flooded bright pink, and my throat tightened in a knot as I became even more embarrassed. I was so stupid! I never should've done that. I should've never even brought him here. It only made me look more foolish.

"I-" I started, closing my eyes. "I'm sorry. I shouldn't have done that."

"No. It's okay," he said.

I sucked in a breath and slowly looked at him. "Then what's wrong?"

He sighed and shook his head. "It's complicated. I do like this place though." He leaned forward to look into the water before asking, "Is it deep enough to swim in?"

I tilted my head at him. He'd changed the subject, which made me send up a silent thank you to God for letting me out of that terribly awkward situation. I looked into the water and shrugged. "It's about as deep as your average pool, I guess. Five feet maybe."

"Wanna take a swim?" he smiled, dazzling me with his mischievous grin.

I giggled and said, "It's a bit too cold for that."

He looked back at the water and nodded. "Someday, then."

Someday. That meant he planned on sticking around for awhile. I hadn't completely screwed up! This made me hopeful that maybe we could be something. Maybe he might even have feelings for me one day, like I was starting to have for him.

That thought made my heart leap from my chest. I had longed to be loved for so long, and the more time I spent with Kaden, talking and just being together, the more something drew me to him. It made me think of us in the future, of us loving one another.

I wasn't a total loser. I had met other guys and spoken to them before, but I'd never felt the vast emotions that I felt towards Kaden. I had to admit that from the moment I'd met him, I'd had feelings for him, despite his cold shoulder. I felt like the jerk attitude he displayed at the beginning was just a wall hiding who he really was. The past few months had proved that, and I wanted so badly to break down that wall completely.

"So," I said, slicing into the silence, "where did you live before you moved here?"

He looked at me and said, "No where exactly. I've been just about everywhere. I never really had a set home."

"So you and your brother are like nomads. Always on the move."

"He's not my brother," he said as his eyes turned away from me.

"Oh," I said. I looked away too. Chewing on my bottom lip, I said, "I'm sorry. That's what he-"

"That's what he told you. Yeah. That's what he tells everyone, but we aren't brothers. He just took me in. He takes a lot of guys like me in."

"Guys like you?" I stared at him, waiting for an answer. He grew stiff next to me, and his eyes became rigid. Tilting his head to glance away from me, he chewed on the inside of his lip. It was obvious from his body language that this was a touchy subject, so I didn't expect him to answer.

He surprised me though when he said, "Someone who doesn't have a family. Someone who has a secret."

His gaze remained far away as he stared across the water. I could see some sort of struggle going on behind his eyes, and his jaw clenched slightly. I swallowed the lump in my throat and dared to ask, "What secret?"

He turned and looked at me. I stared back, peering into his incredibly light blue eyes. I could see he was still fighting with something on the inside. Probably whatever secret he was referring to. He opened his mouth slightly to say something, then closed it again.

He took a deep breath, and just when I thought he was about to tell me, he shook his head. "I can't tell you."

"Oh," I said, not bothering to hide the disappointment in my voice as I turned back to the water.

My shoulders sagged as the blow from his rejection swept through me. I wanted him to confide in me the way I had been confiding in him about everything. This was a chance to do that, but instead, he left me feeling distraught. I sighed before slipping my shoe off and sticking my toes into the water, seeking its calm reassurance.

"But-" he started. He leaned forward slightly to meet my eyes. I looked back at him. "I will tell you someday."

I gave him a half-hearted smile. "Someday."

Chapter Seven

FTER SITTING BY THE pond and talking for what seemed like hours, we finally got up to head into town. We decided to go eat at a tiny restaurant that had a little bit of everything to choose from.

We sat at a nice table in the middle of the room, and I loved the way it felt to be seen with him. Every girl was throwing curious glances our way, clearly deeming him highly attractive, which he was. He was the most handsome guy I had ever seen.

His jet black hair laid just the right way, falling across his long lashes occasionally. The light color of his blue eyes mirrored that of a calm and clear ocean, tossing my nerves about in a never ending wave. All of this, paired with his built figure and perfect smile, made him undeniably beautiful.

I was also a bit happy to see that I was receiving a few appraising glances from guys too. Even so, their looks of approval didn't faze me. Kaden's sweet gaze and warm smile were all I needed.

"You were right," Kaden said, looking around the dimly lit room. "This place looks nice."

"Yeah. I hear the food is pretty good too," I said, picking up the menu to look it over.

"Wait," he said, leaning forward. "You've never actually eaten here?"

I smiled and shook my head. "I've never really had anyone to go out with, so I didn't have a reason to come here. Until now that is."

"Well, if the food sucks, it's on you then," he said with a teasing smirk. I rolled my eyes, and he gave me that grin again. Every time he smiled at me like that, it sent sweet shivers down my arms, and it made my stomach do backflips.

I looked to my left as the waitress approached our table, and when her eyes fell on Kaden, I watched her perk up. She bit her lip and tucked her auburn hair behind her ear. The corners of her mouth lifted in a small smile, and she started batting her long lashes. She was trying to look good for him! She clearly didn't seem to care that he was out with me. I mean granted, she was beautiful, so she must have thought she could just steal him away.

"Hi!" she smiled as she reached our table. She didn't address me when she said it. She only looked at him. "Can I get you something to drink?"

Kaden looked at her and to my enjoyment, he didn't seem affected by her smile or the way she looked at him. He didn't return her friendliness, but instead just looked at her to ask, "Do you have sweet tea?"

"Of course! Anything for you!" She rested her notepad

below her breasts in an attempt to push them up more as she wrote his drink down. Still smiling, she glanced at him to see if he was noticing. I glared at her, and my cheeks grew fiery hot. Despite my trying to remain calm, her efforts were really bugging me.

Kaden seemed to notice my reaction to her, so he said, "No. That's not what I want. I just wanted to know if you had it."

She seemed taken aback by this and confused, but she just kept smiling. "Oh, okay. What would you like then sir?"

"I'll have whatever my beautiful date has," he said, looking at me with a smile. I knew I was grinning from ear to ear and blushing like a mad fool, but I didn't care! He thought I was beautiful, and he was turning down this attractive girl. These moments we kept sharing and times when he did things like this all had me falling for him. It was getting harder to deny how I felt.

She looked at me with an annoyed expression and asked in a monotone voice, "What do you want?"

"Sweet tea," I said without hesitating.

She wrote it down and left in a huff. I looked at Kaden and laughed. "She wasn't too friendly. What made you do that?"

"Do what?" he smiled.

"Mess with her and tell her I was your-" I blushed again, "you know, your beautiful date."

"Well, that's what you are, aren't you?" He raised his eyebrows and stared at me. I could only smile and nod.

After our waitress brought us our teas and took our

order for food, I excused myself to the bathroom. I walked in and looked at my reflection in the mirror. My curls seemed fuller tonight, and my jet black hair seemed shinier. My cheeks had a nice rosiness to them, and my lips matched. My emerald eyes had a glimmer to them that I had never seen before. I really did look beautiful. It felt nice.

I looked down at the sink and started to wash my hands when I realized something smelled like smoke. I turned off the water and sniffed. A thick, smoldering scent filled the air, and it hit me hard. It *really* smelled like something was burning. I looked in each of the stalls to see if there was a source for the smell in them, but there was no sign of anything on fire.

I figured it was probably someone in the kitchen burning food, but as soon as that thought occurred to me, screaming erupted in the restaurant, followed by dozens of running footsteps. My heart stopped as I ran to the door to get out of there, like everyone else. There must be a fire! I pulled on the door, but it wouldn't budge. I tried again, but nothing happened.

Someone had locked it from the outside.

My heart sped up as smoke started coming into the bathroom from outside. My fists beat hard on the door as I cried and screamed for help. I knew no one would come though. The footsteps had disappeared, which meant everyone was probably outside already. No one knew I was trapped in here, except maybe Kaden. Even so, I couldn't wait on him or anyone else.

I needed to get out of here before the place burnt down

or I suffocated, so I took a few steps back from the door and threw my body up against it in an attempt to bust it down. The door remained firm in its place, but I refused to give up. Taking even more steps back from the door, I ran at it harder. My left side slammed into the metal, but it still didn't budge. I had to clutch my arm though as pain shot up it. Tears streamed down my cheeks as the heavy black smoke filled the bathroom. The door had heated up by this point too, so I was forced to back away from it. The thick smoke was burning my throat and eyes, so I closed them and got on the floor.

"Help!" I screamed as loud as my lungs would allow. It was getting harder to breathe, and I was starting to get dizzy. The room was spinning as I tried to inhale, but I only choked on more smoke.

I crawled to the far wall of the bathroom and leaned my head against it. My body racked with painful coughs as the smoke billowed around me. I couldn't open my eyes anymore. I tried covering my mouth and nose with the top of my dress, but it was no use. I was engulfed in smoke.

I laid flat on the floor, and I could feel sparks of heat edging closer to me. My tear stained face was becoming hot as I accepted the reality of my situation. This would be it for me. I was going to die. By suffocation or burning, I didn't know. I was just thankful that these last few months had been happy ones because of Kaden, and I hoped that he was safe outside. Maybe at least he would mourn my being gone.

"Kaden," I coughed.

That's when I felt hands grab me and scoop me up. I

still couldn't open my eyes because the smoke was so thick and dark. It consumed everything around it, so I held on with what little strength I had to whoever it was that held me. My rescuer cradled me against their chest as they ran out of the bathroom. They clutched me tightly in a steady hold as their movements became rushed and jagged in an attempt to escape the flames.

When we finally made it outside I attempted to take in a large gulp of fresh air, but it was still painful and difficult. My lungs were filled with the toxic smoke. I tried to open my eyes, but it burnt to the point that I didn't want to move. The person who clutched me tightly to their chest was breathing hard, and the feel of their warm breath kissed my cheeks.

I blinked a couple of times after being away from the burning building for a few moments. My eyes watered as I forced them to open, and tears dripped out of both corners. The salty drops rolled down the sides of my face as I finally pried my eyes open enough to see.

Kaden's blurry face hovered above me, so I blinked the tears and burning sensation away. After a few blinks, his features became clear, but as soon as I saw his troubled gaze, I wished I'd kept my eyes shut. He was looking down into my eyes with worry behind his stare, and it was etched into every part of him.

"Thank God you're okay!" he said, hugging me tightly. Relief flooded his face as his brow unfurrowed, and the hard line of his mouth quivered slightly.

I coughed and wheezed more, wishing I could hug him

back, but I could barely breathe, let alone move my arms. That's when the fire trucks arrived with an ambulance right behind them. Kaden ran over to them, and he carefully passed my limp body to the EMTs.

My eyes slipped closed once more, and I could feel myself start to drift away as they placed an oxygen mask on me. Darkness swirled all around my head, and I wanted to succumb to its greedy hands. I struggled to fight it as I inhaled the fresh air, allowing it to travel through my lungs.

Lying there, I breathed in and out, just bathing in the sweet feeling of being able to breathe again. When I opened my eyes, Kaden was still there, looking down at me. I gave him a small smile, but he probably couldn't even tell due to the mask.

"She's okay, right?" Kaden looked to a fireman and EMT.

"She doesn't appear to have any burns, which is very good," the EMT said as his eyes searched all over my body and clothing. "She should be fine as long as she keeps breathing that for a few more minutes. Then she needs to get home to get some rest and drink plenty of water."

"I'll get her home. Thank you for helping her." Kaden looked back down at me and gently took my hand. The gesture was warm, and the feeling of his touch soothed me inside and out.

"Son, don't thank us," the fireman said. "You're the one that saved her. A group of people said that you ran back in when you realized she wasn't outside."

Kaden nodded.

"That takes a lot of guts. She must mean a lot to you."

Kaden looked back down at me. We stared at each other for a long time. He'd saved me. He'd risked his life to come back and get me. At that moment, my heart went to him. I wasn't going to deny my feelings for him anymore. He was all I wanted. I'd never expected anything like this from anyone. This kind of act made me really wonder just what I meant to him.

He continued to watch me with caring eyes, and he softly brushed a strand of my hair back from my forehead to tuck it behind my ear. I closed my eyes and pushed my cheek closer into the palm of his hand. His touch sent a surge of calm and safety through me. I wanted to feel that way forever.

When I finally felt like I could breathe on my own again, they all helped me to sit up slowly. The EMT asked me a couple of questions, like my name and where I was, just to be sure I hadn't suffered from any brain damage. When I was able to tell him what he needed to know, they said that I was free to go home.

Kaden slipped his arm around my waist to help me stand as we headed in the direction of my house. When we'd walked a few blocks from the restaurant, my legs started growing weak again. The night was catching up to me, and everything felt harder. Walking, standing, even keeping my eyes open. My body was exhausted.

Kaden must have sensed this change in me as well because he scooped me up in his arms as if I weighed nothing. He clutched me tightly to his chest and kissed me softly on the forehead. My skin warmed. I smiled and leaned my head on his shoulder, feeling happier than I ever had in my whole entire life.

"I can't thank you enough for saving me," I said, looking up into his blue eyes. Tears began to brim over my eyes and down onto my cheeks once more as I whispered, "I really thought I was going to die in there."

"I won't ever let anything happen to you Raven. No more getting hurt or attacked in any way."

He stared directly in my eyes, and I knew he was telling the truth. His gaze was strong and unwavering with his promise to me. I knew he would protect me, and I silently vowed to do the same for him. If ever a time came when he needed saving, I would be there to protect him. I pushed my face closer into the crook of his neck and breathed in his musky, intoxicating scent. A happy shiver ran through me.

"Why do you care about me so much?" I asked.

"I have my reasons," he smiled.

"Can you tell me what they are?"

He looked away from me to stare forward. Grinning, he nodded. "Someday."

When we got to my house, I told Kaden I didn't want to go in through the front door because I didn't want to deal with my dad. He understood, so he took me over to my bedroom window.

I slid it open, and he helped me climb in before following suit. I went over to my bedroom door and shut it quietly before I turned back to Kaden. He was standing in the middle of my dark room, watching me.

I swallowed, nervous at the reality of having him in my room. I ducked my eyes and whispered, "Thank you for bringing me home and for saving me tonight. I'm sorry that the date was ruined. Maybe we can try again soon."

I had left my bedroom light off, so the only source of light came from the moon outside. He looked amazing with the pure light of the moon behind his dark figure. It outlined him with a white silhouette, and the contrast between it and his dark hair and clothes was stunning. The image gave him an almost magical feel. It was probably the most beautiful thing I had ever seen.

"Of course," he said with a smile. His eyes traced my body from head to toe as he asked, "Do you need help changing?"

I stared at him head on and put my hands on my hips. He laughed in a hushed tone before saying, "I'm kidding."

I smiled and walked to stand right in front of him. "Really? Because I was going to say yes." He frowned, so it was my turn to laugh. "Kidding," I said, still smiling.

"I know," he said, tucking my hair behind my ear in a loving gesture. He leaned forward and kissed my forehead once more. "Goodnight, Raven."

I walked back to the window with him as he climbed out of it. He looked back over his shoulder to smile at me before walking away. I couldn't stop smiling as I stood at the window, staring at him as he walked in the direction of his home. He had me in a blissfully happy mood, even after what had just happened. He was turning out to be the answer to my prayers. I was starting to believe that what we had could be actual love.

I sighed as I lost myself in lively thoughts of us and the potential for the future. When he was finally out of my sight, I continued to smile as I whispered, "Goodnight, Kaden."

Chapter Eight

THE NEXT MORNING, I was beyond ready to go to school. I couldn't wait to see Kaden again. After how he responded to my dressing up yesterday, I decided to actually wear something nice. I threw on a tight shirt that showed off my chest and some jeans that I thought my butt looked amazing in. I decided to leave my hair down instead of forcing it into a ponytail. It fell all the way down my back in beautiful waves of onyx. I gave my reflection a satisfied grin before darting away towards school.

All day I waited in anticipation for English. I couldn't wait to see Kaden smile at me again and to hear the soothing sound of his voice as he spoke. He was doing crazy things to my heart, and I could barely contain my smile all day long.

It was strange though. I seemed to be getting more looks from guys who usually just ignored my existence. Anytime I passed by a guy, he'd smile at me or even whistle occasionally. I would always give them a polite smile back, but no matter how many of them noticed me, I didn't care.

I only wanted Kaden.

When it was time for last block, I nearly ran to English. Kaden wasn't there yet when I walked in, so I calmed myself down and began walking towards my chair. As I reached the aisle that led to my seat, I had to stop when a guy named Simon stepped in my way.

Simon was the guy most of the girls at the school swooned over and went for. He had a brown pompadour hairstyle, charming green eyes, and a well-known smile that lured every girl in to him. But I'd personally never understood the obsession with him.

"Hi there," he said, giving me a devilish grin.

I took a step back, thrown off by his sudden approach. I looked to my left at the girls he had just been flirting with. They seemed pretty confused too. And pissed.

"Hi?" I said, not even bothering to hide the confusion in my voice. I squinted my eyes and tilted my head a little, not understanding why he was talking to me. Simon never talked to me, and I was pretty sure he never even looked in my direction either.

"I'm Simon. Are you new here?"

I narrowed my eyes and crossed my arms. "No? I've gone here forever. I'm Raven. The girl who sits in the back."

His eyes opened wide, and he looked at me from head to toe. A smile lit his face again as he said, "Damn, Raven! You clean up good. This new look works for you."

I looked down at myself. The curves of my breasts were in full view, and my figure stood out due to the form fitting shirt and jeans. I suddenly felt self-conscious. When I'd put this outfit on, I hadn't thought about all the other attention that could come with it. Not that it didn't make me feel pretty, because it did. Before Kaden, no one had ever told me I looked good in something, but still, I didn't want the way I looked to be the only reason someone was into me.

"Listen," he said, "I know we haven't really talked much-"

"Ever. We haven't talked ever."

He continued as if not hearing me. "-but maybe you and I could go out sometime."

His lips curled into that famous smile of his, which was known to have drawn every girl he flashed it at into his arms. Simon's reputation was huge. Even someone with no social skills like me had heard the stories about him.

After he and a girl went out, he would get what he needed from them just to drop them and never speak again. Well, that was unless they were good at what he wanted. Those girls he kept around for times when he didn't have dates.

"This Friday maybe?" he asked

I was so taken off guard by this that I lost my voice for a moment. Amazed, I stared at him with my mouth hung open slightly. He wanted to take me out? This guy who hadn't even realized I was in the same room as him for a whole semester wanted to take me out on a date? This made me so angry that my whole face lit up smoldering red. How dare he be so conceited and shallow!

"Sorry, but I'm seeing someone," I said, and there was a hint of venom in my voice.

I didn't know how much truth that statement held, but I didn't care. I didn't want to go out with Simon. I liked Kaden, and I only wanted to be with him. Ever since I'd seen him, there was something about him that had awoken a warm spark within me. He made me feel a string of elated emotions inside, and I loved the way it felt.

I loved the way *he* made me feel.

I went to push past Simon when he grabbed my arm. I whipped my head around to glare at him as he turned me back to face him. "Who are you seeing?"

"That's none of your business," I said, narrowing my eyes further.

I tugged my arm away from him and stormed to my seat. Still livid about Simon's behavior, I sat down with a huff. I urged my body to take calm, steadying breaths in an attempt to keep my anger at bay. He stared at me for another moment with a smirk playing at his lips. When he was satisfied with looking in my direction, he returned to talking to the two girls whom he had been with before he so rudely ruined my mood.

What a pig!

I turned away from him to look at the door of the classroom. Switching my focus from Simon to Kaden's arrival replaced my boiling anger with a fidgety excitement. Class started in five minutes, and I felt my palms get sweaty in anticipation. I couldn't wait to see him! I tried to act natural by looking away from the door every now and then, but it was so hard to not be excited.

When I looked at the clock again, my excitement

started to dwindle. There was only a minute left before class started. I looked back at the door, and my anticipation turned to worry. Where was he? Was he going to be late?

The bell rang, making my heart sink, and Mr. Brooks started the lesson for the day. The more he talked, the lower my heart sunk. He wasn't coming. Kaden wasn't coming.

I looked down at the revealing outfit I was wearing, and I wanted to kick myself for being an idiot. This was what I got for trying to look good! I had worn this, made myself look stupid, and only got let down. I crossed my arms over myself to hide my body. My cheeks burned, and I closed my eyes in embarrassment. What had I been thinking by putting this on?

When class ended, I hurried outside to head home. I wanted away from the school and away from this day. Once I was halfway across the school parking lot, the sound of someone yelling my name forced me to pause. Knowing who it was, I stopped walking to turn around.

"What, Simon?"

He slowed once he stood in front of me. He smiled as he panted from jogging over to me. "Look," he started, "I'm sorry for what I said in there. That was really shitty of me. How about I make it up to you by driving you home?" He smiled even bigger, no doubt trying to make me fall for him. Too bad that I had already fallen for someone else.

"I told you that I'm already seeing someone."

He frowned. "Is he driving you home today?"

I looked all around for Kaden. A glimpse of his crystal blue eyes, strands of his dark hair blowing in the wind, anything. I just needed to see him, but of course, he still wasn't anywhere in sight. I matched Simon's turned down mouth, and I shrugged my shoulders. "Well, no. He wasn't here today."

"Great," he smiled once more. "I'll do the honors then."

I backed away and faked a polite smile since obvious rejection didn't seem to work on him. "I prefer to walk home. Thank you for the offer though."

Before he could object, I turned and ran towards home. My legs burned from running, and the wind kissed my nose, making it icy cold. I didn't slow down until I came to my trailer. I trudged to the front door. Leaning against it, I breathed hard and braced my hands on my legs.

A twig snapped in the woods to my right, and a shiver ran through me at the sound. I jumped to stand up straight, turning to face the large expanse of forest. My heart sped up as I searched the darkened trees for the source of the sound. My breathing was still heavy as I strained my eyes to look as hard as they possibly could. I couldn't be sure, but it felt like someone was hiding in those shadows. I could sense someone or something there, and a prickling sensation traveled up the back of my neck as I felt their eyes on me. When I heard another twig snap, I didn't stick around to look anymore. I ran inside and locked the door behind me.

As the adrenaline left my body, I limped to my room, exhausted. When I got to my room, I closed the door behind me and shut my eyes. Leaning against it, I willed myself to calm down. Everything had me on edge. I had become so paranoid after everything that had gone on. The only time I was ever able to forget being afraid was when Kaden was near. He made me feel protected and cared for in a way I never had before. I missed him, but thinking of him only brought on more sorrow.

Opening my eyes, I finally calmed my breathing down to a normal level. I went to my closet to grab a t-shirt and hoodie for work. As I grabbed the hem of my shirt to pull it off, I glanced in the mirror at my reflection. I really did look good. This outfit hugged me in all the right places, and the shirt hung dangerously low. If Kaden had seen me dressed in this, he would've gone wild.

With that in mind, I nodded in determination. I wanted Kaden to see me this way. I wanted to make him lose his mind when he saw the way I looked. I was always the one expressing my emotions, so for once, I wanted him to slip up. I wanted to see his raw, unfiltered reaction to me. I would dress this way again tomorrow, and if he wasn't at school, then I would do it the next day and the next.

Still looking in the mirror, I caught movement behind me. I glanced at it through the reflection, and that's when I saw Kaden peering in. I spun around to face the window, but nothing was there. Running to it, I threw it open and gazed out. He was nowhere in sight.

The side of the trailer that held my room faced towards an open field, so there was nowhere he could have hidden. I had also reached my window fairly quickly, so there was no way he could have run out of my sight either. My mind must have been playing tricks on me. A cruel, sick trick.

I sighed before coming back into my room. Shutting

the window and curtain, I changed into the casual clothes I had pulled from the closet. I grabbed my bag and left my room to walk to the bookstore. Hugging my arms to my body, I tried to stay warm the whole way there.

It was times like these, when it was dark and cold, that I wished I had a car. My dad's old Malibu would be a fine car to drive, but he'd let it get so far gone that it hadn't worked in years. On top of that, and I mean literally on top, a tree had fallen on it in the side driveway, so it wasn't going anywhere.

When I got to work, I busied myself with pointless tasks or read my book. I would glance at the door every now and then, expecting Kaden to walk through it just like he had been doing for the past few months. It hadn't dawned on me until now just how much Kaden's presence had become a part of my life.

For months, I'd seen him every day without fail. We'd laughed and talked about anything and everything, and even in the moments where we'd been silent, our eyes had continued to dance in each other's gaze. He was a part of me now, so I couldn't help but search for him. I had no such luck in seeing him though. He never came in or walked by.

I sighed as the sky changed from blue to a mix of orange and pink, before finally resting on black. It was nightfall, which meant it was time to head home. I closed up the shop and made a point to hurry home. I still didn't like being on the streets by myself at night. I tried walking in the middle of the street when cars weren't going by so I wouldn't have to walk by the alleys alone. I didn't have the courage to do it.

When I finally made it home, I walked in, feeling hollow inside. I had built up so much anticipation and excitement at the thought of seeing Kaden, and all of those emotions just left me all at once. The only thing left was a sad, dark void in the pit of my stomach.

I looked up to walk to my room and saw my dad lying face down on the floor. My stomach jumped into my throat as I dropped my bags and ran to his side. Fear squeezed at my heart as I crouched down next to him. I slowly rolled him over, my heart beating ferociously. Tears brimmed in my eyes as I checked for breathing. His chest was rising and falling.

I let out a sigh of relief as it settled in that he was still alive. He had a gash on his forehead from where he had fallen, but other than that, I didn't see any visible signs of injury. He started mumbling to himself about needing another drink, and I took that as a sign that he was perfectly fine. He had just passed out from being so drunk.

"What am I going to do with you?" I mumbled to myself with a heavy sigh.

I shook my head in frustration as I moved to stand up. Stepping near his head to grab him under the arms, I dragged him onto the carpet in the living room. My muscles strained under his weight, and it took everything in me not to topple over him.

I finally managed to get him onto the soft carpet, where I placed a pillow under his head and covered him with a throw blanket. If he woke up in his old bedroom, he would have a fit because that room only reminded him of my mom, so I knew better than to take him there. The living room carpet was the next best option, seeing that we didn't have a couch, and there was no way that I could lift him into his recliner.

He started snoring once I finished getting him settled, and I felt my heart begin to ache. That was supposed to be me. He was supposed to take care of me and tuck me in, not the other way around. He was supposed to be my dad, the man who picked me up when I fell or kissed my bruises when I managed to hurt myself. I was supposed to be his little girl, but I wasn't. I was nothing.

I walked away to my room, crying softly from all the frustration, exhaustion, and loneliness that coursed through me. Shutting the door, I crawled into bed with my entire being feeling defeated. I wished more than anything that things were different. I wanted and needed somebody. I wanted and needed Kaden.

With him, I forgot all of the bad things. With him, breathing didn't feel as difficult or painful. When I was with him, I experienced the bliss that came with smiling and laughing in endless fits. Being with him, I was able to remember I wasn't alone. He was there for me. With thoughts of him still filling my head, I finally fell asleep, but even then, I didn't stop thinking of him.

I knew I was dreaming, but I was in the same spot and position in my bed that I'd fallen asleep in. I lied there, staring at my window as Kaden climbed in through it. He straightened at the foot of my bed and looked at me with his beautiful blue eyes. His dark hair fell across his face as he stared at me for a moment. I smiled at him, which made him slowly approach the side of my bed. Lowering himself onto it, he laid down next to me. I smiled even bigger as he put his arm around me and brought me closer, our bodies pressing together.

"Where were you today?" I asked in a quiet voice as my stomach did flips. His body was so warm against mine, and his arm felt so strong and secure.

He had a pained expression on his face as he shut his eyes. Leaning down, he pressed his forehead to mine and whispered, "I'm so sorry." The words came out strained, and his voice had a desperate catch to it. Something told me his apology had a much deeper meaning to it. There was something very wrong.

I swallowed hard, feeling knots in my stomach. "You're sorry? For what, Kaden? Tell me what's wrong. Please. Let me help you." I reached up and tangled my fingers into the back of his hair as tears welled up in my eyes. "Please, Kaden."

He gave a soft smile and pulled back to look into my eyes. "You're always wanting to help people. Like your dad. You shouldn't have to help him, Raven. That's not your job." He looked away from me then and said, "It's not your job to help me either. I was supposed to be doing that for you, but I failed."

He looked back at me as a tear rolled down my cheek. Carefully, he wiped it away with his thumb. His usual bright eyes and glowing smile were turned down in a mask of agony as he stared at me, watching the tears drip down my face. He inhaled a deep breath then whispered, "Please, be safe, and remember that I'm sorry."

He pulled his hand away and got up out of the bed. I sat up as he walked back towards the window with his shoulders hunched over. I quickly jumped to my feet in a desperate attempt to follow him to the window. He couldn't leave, not yet.

When he was about to climb out, I grabbed him by the arm and pleaded, "Tell me what's going on!"

He didn't look back at me as he pulled his arm away from me. He crawled out the window, his figure blending in with the darkness of the night. I went to move after him, but an unseen force rooted my body to the ground. I looked down at my frozen feet, and frustration hit me. No matter how much I struggled against the invisible hold, I couldn't move. Only after Kaden's image vanished did I regain control of my body.

When I caught up to the fact that I could move again, I raced the rest of the way to the window, leaning all the way out. He was gone. He'd left me behind. Warm tears spilled over as I walked back to my bed. Why did my body and mind have to torture me? This wasn't a dream. This was a nightmare.

Chapter Nine

WHEN I WOKE UP the next morning, I could taste the saltiness of tears and feel the cool trails they had taken down my cheeks. I had been crying in my sleep. I sat up slowly and looked at my window. It was open, and the curtain billowed in the cold morning air. I could've sworn it was shut last night.

I breathed in as I caught a scent in the air that made my heart constrict. It smelt like Kaden, a sweet, musky smell. I knew it must be my mind playing tricks on me, so I dashed out of my room to go shower. I couldn't let myself just sit there and cry. After all, that was just a dream, not real life. I would get ready for the day and, hopefully, see Kaden once English began.

I dressed in a tight, long sleeved black top that revealed about the same amount of my chest as yesterday, maybe even a little more. With it, I wore a pair of dark skinny jeans, and I let my hair cascade down my back. I applied a shiny layer of lip gloss in order to make my lips shine, and when I looked into the mirror, I was more than satisfied with my appearance. I looked good. I nodded, ready for the day.

I went through the motions of the day, moving from class to class, while receiving stares from many guys and even some females. I smiled at myself, sure that when Kaden saw me, he would not be able to stop staring. The thought of his reaction made me giddy.

When it grew time for English, I approached the classroom, breathing in and out slowly. I had to remain calm. When I walked in, I noticed that Kaden wasn't there yet. My heart sunk, but I didn't lose hope. He could still show up. I made my way to my desk and sat down, but as soon as I did, Simon approached.

"Hey there," he said as he sat down at Kaden's desk.

"That seat is taken," I said, glaring at him.

He smiled and asked, "By who? The guy you're seeing?"

"Yes, actually." I crossed my arms and nodded.

"So you're with the new guy?" I nodded, and he laughed. Raising an eyebrow at me, he wore a cocky smirk. "You could do so much better than that goth guy."

"Oh yeah?" I sneered at him. "Like who?"

"Like me. I'm way better than him. You'll figure that out sooner or later. They all do."

The minute bell rang, and he looked at the clock. When he turned away, I wanted more than anything to take my textbook and slap him across the side of his head with it, but I restrained myself. No need to waste energy on this idiot.

When he faced me again, he smiled and said, "Think about my offer of taking you out. I guarantee that you'll have a much better time with me than that loser."

"He isn't-" I didn't get to finish my words because he stood and walked to his desk.

I groaned, and the urge to throw my textbook at the back of his head flashed through my mind again. How dare he judge Kaden? He didn't even know him. He had no right to speak to me that way about things that he didn't even know. Kaden wasn't a loser, and I was positive that I could never have a better time with Simon than with Kaden.

My thoughts were drowned out by the sound of the bell signifying the beginning of class. My eyes flicked to the door, then to the empty seat next to mine. No Kaden. I closed my eyes and slumped down in my chair. I felt deflated as I kept saying to myself, *Kaden isn't coming*.

I suddenly started playing out all the scenarios that could have resulted in him not being here in my head. What if the smoke from the restaurant had poisoned him, and he was sick? After all, he'd never gotten treated, even though he had been in the fire too. What if the smoke had done something to him, and he was hurt? Or worse, what if he was dead?

I squirmed in my chair as I pushed that thought out of my head. I wouldn't think that way. I *couldn't* think that way. Kaden wasn't dead. He was probably just sick. It was moments like this that made me wish I had a phone so I could contact him. Even better, I wish I knew where he lived, so I could go check to see if he was okay. Maybe if I saw Landon around town, I could ask him how Kaden was, but who knew when I was going to see him again.

I shook my head in an attempt to calm down. I didn't need to stress over this. Looking back to Mr. Brooks, who was speaking about William Shakespeare, I tried to ignore the tornado of emotions sailing through me. It was pointless though. No matter how hard I tried, I couldn't stop worrying about Kaden and all of the possible reasons for his absence.

When the bell finally rang, I found it difficult to stand up and make my way home. I walked slowly, with my head down. My stomach was twisted in worried knots. I had no way of knowing exactly what was going on, and after Kaden had done so much to take care of me, I wanted to do the same for him. I'd promised myself I would protect him, but how could I do that when I didn't even know where he was or what was wrong? Since I didn't have the luxury of knowing any of that information, all I could do was wait.

I pulled my arms tighter around myself as I distanced myself away from the school. I turned the corner of the woods that led toward my house before coming face to face with Kaden. I gasped upon running into him before being overtaken by joy and relief.

"Kaden!" I hugged him, smiling from ear to ear. All of my fears vanished in an instant. He was here with me! He was right in front of me! "I was so worried about you!"

He grabbed me by the shoulders and pulled me off him. He was sneering at me with disgust written all over his face. I squinted my eyes at him, confused as to why he was staring at me like that.

Before I could say anything, he said, "I never want to see you again."

I blinked, trying to clear the fogginess out of my head. I was sure I'd misunderstood his words. "What? What do you mean?"

"Exactly what I said. I never want to see you again."

My throat clenched up, and the world began to tilt. I shook my head, feeling hot tears well up in my eyes. "How can you say that?"

"Easy," he said with a grin, but this one wasn't out of kindness. Cruelty was written all over his face, and he shoved his hands into his front jean pockets as if we were having a casual conversation. "I can't believe you thought I cared about you. You actually fell for it."

I shook my head slowly, refusing to believe his words. *This isn't real.* This wasn't happening. He wouldn't say these things to me. Kaden had to have cared about me somewhat. Right? We had spent so much time together, and all of the smiles, laughs, and feelings felt so real. Not just for me, but for him too. That couldn't be a lie. It just couldn't. Whether he had meant it in a romantic sense or not, his friendship couldn't be a lie.

"I never cared about you, Raven. How could anyone care about someone so miserable and pathetic?" He gave me a once over, taking in what I was wearing. He scowled, and his disgusted eyes narrowed further. Curling his lip to sneer at me, he asked, "What are you wearing? Did you do that to impress me?" He threw his head back and laughed. When he calmed down, he looked back at me, still smiling. "That is so pitiful."

I turned away as his words cut into me. Never had I been so hurt. His words stung more than any cut or bruise I had ever received. This was a pain that clawed at me inside, breaking my heart in two. It was eating away at me, and my chest felt constricted.

Tears rolled down my cheeks as I demanded, "Then why save me at the restaurant, huh? Why not let me burn? If you didn't care then what was the point in risking your life to come get me out?"

He shrugged and said, "Added more to the joke. Made you fall harder, which only amuses me more."

I was so hurt and confused by all of this that all I could do was look away from him and cry. My mind raced to figure out how this could be happening. How could he say these things to me when only days ago he behaved as though there was something there between us? He wasn't acting then either. His eyes told me how genuine he was in all of those sweet moments, so this had to be something else. His words and actions then had me believing he cared. I thought he actually wanted to be with me, but now he was acting like the biggest jerk I had ever met. Even more so than Simon.

I opened my eyes as the thought of Simon gave me an idea.

"Well," I started, glaring at him as I angrily brushed the tears away from my eyes. "The joke is on you because I've actually already found someone else. Someone better than you."

His cocky smile slowly fell as he said through gritted teeth, "What do you mean?"

"Exactly what I said, Kaden," I sneered, mocking his words. "I'm with Simon now."

He suddenly lunged at me, pinning me against a tree. His body moved at an incredible speed, and I had no time to see, let alone react to him. He held me there against the rough tree trunk with one arm against my chest and the other holding both of my hands behind my back. I breathed in and out rapidly, knowing that I should be frightened, but I wasn't. Something told me that he wouldn't actually hurt me, so I held my ground. I stared back up at him, meeting his chilling stare.

"You can't be with Simon."

"And just why not?" I got up in his face, demanding an answer. He leaned forward, making me draw back to avoid his face from touching mine. Our lips had nearly touched.

"He only wants one thing, Raven."

"You mean like you?" I was breathing heavy again as he recoiled slightly. I had thrown his words back at him, and he knew I had him cornered. "Every guy only cares about sex, remember?"

"Simon is different though. He will strictly use you for that and that alone."

"Well maybe I want that too!"

He laughed, loosening his grip on me. He stepped back from me, allowing me to lean freely against the tree. Crossing his arms over his chest, he said with a smug expression, "You don't want sex."

"How would you know? You didn't stick around long enough to find out!"

My heart was racing a mile a minute, and I could feel tears trying to come out again. I refused to let them this time.

I had to hold my ground. My body was shaking from the amount of anger coursing through me. I still couldn't believe that this was happening.

More than anything, I wanted to rewind to when we were happy and he was acting normal. His behavior was so sudden and hurtful. He didn't seem at all like who I thought he was. Then again, maybe I had let my feelings blind me from who he really was. Maybe I wanted to make myself see something that wasn't really there.

"Fine," he said. "Be with Simon. Like I said, I don't care."

"Good," I huffed, "because we're going out Friday."

He balled his fist up and tightened his jaw. "Great. Have fun."

He turned to walk away from me, but after only a step, he froze. He let out an aggravated growl as he quickly spun back around. He grabbed me by the shoulders and said, "If he tries anything with you, makes one wrong move, hurts you, or comes after you in any way, I will be there."

We held each other's gaze as he released his grip on my arms. He turned away from me and walked towards town. I stood there, watching him leave with my heart in my throat. When I could no longer see him, I ran the rest of the way home crying.

Why did he have to be so confusing? Did he care or didn't he? Everything about him was so puzzling, and I had no experience to go off of to determine if this was normal or not. I just wanted to know what was going on and what I had done wrong.

This was not the same guy I had gone out with. It couldn't be. Something wasn't right, but there was nothing I could do right now. All I could do was act out my plan at getting to Kaden. He could deny it, but I knew my going out with Simon bothered him. It was the perfect way to show him how he was making me feel, and to see how he felt about me. If he got jealous, I would know that he did have feelings for me, which would mean everything he'd just said was a lie.

If that was the case, I needed to figure out what was really going on. There was more to this than what he was letting on, and I was determined to figure out just what it was.

Chapter Ten

A S SOON AS ENGLISH began the next day, I knew exactly what to do. I let myself remember all the pain that Kaden caused me the day before with his words. I let it boil over inside of me, making me as angry as humanly possible. That was the only way I could actually go through with this plan. When I was at my breaking point, I walked into the classroom and made my way straight to Simon's desk.

He was sitting on the edge of it, talking to some strawberry blond girl with his charming smile. I stepped between them to stand directly in front of him. His wide eyes took me in from head to toe, and his grin told me just how pleased he was with what he saw.

I had worn the sluttiest outfit I owned, which happened to be a tight mini skirt with fishnet tights and a tank top that revealed the curves of my chest and part of my stomach. I'm pretty sure that it wasn't even within the school dress code, but none of my teachers seemed to notice, so they didn't tell me to change. The only bad part about it was that it was freezing outside, so I felt like a popsicle.

When Simon's eyes made it back to mine after giving me a double take, I smiled at him and asked, "When were you wanting to go out?"

He gave me a devilish grin and said, "Tomorrow night?"

"Sounds good." I blew him a kiss just to add to the act before sitting down at the desk next to his.

This shocked everyone around us, but what shocked them more was my outfit. I'd never worn this kind of thing out in public, let alone in school. I only owned the clothes because they were part of my Halloween costume from the year before, so when the people around me saw how I looked, they were stunned. A few guys in the class left to come sit in a seat near mine, and I gave each and every one of them a smile that matched Simon's. They could hardly contain themselves.

When class was about to start, my stomach fell as Kaden walked in. His face was expressionless as he came into the classroom, but that changed when his eyes fell on me and all the guys I had around me. Something dark crossed his face, and I knew I had struck a nerve. He was jealous, but I wasn't even close to being done.

I looked away from him, flipping my hair over my shoulder, and I leaned even lower onto the desk to expose more of my breasts to all the guys. Each of them leaned closer with eager eyes, and they started firing offers to take me out.

"Sorry boys," Simon said, pulling his desk closer to mine. He draped his arm around my shoulder and leaned back in his seat. "She and I are hanging out."

All of the guys seemed very disappointed by this. They groaned and moved further back from us. It was as if Simon was the ringleader that they all respected, so they stepped down, allowing me to be claimed as his. I looked at Simon to give him a half-hearted smile. My plan was working, so I should've been happy. The longer it went on though, the worse I felt. Swallowing hard, I glanced towards Kaden.

He was still standing by the door watching us, except it wasn't me he was looking at. He was staring at Simon in a way I had never seen him look before. Angry didn't even come close to the look he had. His eyes turned dark as they bore into Simon, and the area surrounding Kaden turned ominous. His hands were clenched into tight, shaking fists, and his lip was curled up in a snarl. I swallowed hard, actually afraid. Only, I wasn't afraid for myself. I feared for Simon's safety.

Simon looked at Kaden with a cocky chuckle before turning back to me. He slid his finger under my chin and made me look at him. "Looks like goth boy is a bit jealous. Did you break his heart, darlin'?" He faked a southern drawl, still smiling into my eyes.

I glanced back at Kaden, allowing Simon to continue holding his finger where it was. I sighed as Kaden spun around in a furious huff, stomping out of the classroom. "Something like that."

I turned away from Simon as Mr. Brooks entered the room. Class started, but my mind had wandered off. I stared at my notebook, making meaningless lines in the margin.

Simon had no idea how far off he was. I hadn't broken Kaden's heart. He had broken mine.

When class was over, Simon walked me out. I quickly found myself bored and irritated, because the entire time he only talked about how good of a baseball player he was. "Like I'm probably the best pitcher in the history of this school! Probably even this state! I have a wicked hit too. Again, the best in the school."

He was grinning, and I smiled back, pretending that I was impressed. Really I just wanted to slap that grin off his face. More than anything, I just wanted to go home to get out of these ridiculous clothes. I had made Kaden jealous. The job was done, and it was obvious to me now that he liked me. I didn't need to push the charade on any longer, but I felt like Kaden seeing me in class with Simon wasn't enough. I needed him to know that I was serious about going on a date with Simon. That way he would come back to me and explain his behavior, hopefully, with an apology alongside his explanation. This was the only way to push Kaden into action.

"That sounds very impressive." I tried to hide the sarcasm, and luckily, Simon didn't hear it. I wasn't really paying attention anymore as Simon continued to talk. My eyes traced all of the surroundings in the parking lot for any sign of Kaden, but I didn't see him anywhere.

When we reached Simon's car, he leaned against it to face me. With a large smile plastered on his face, he asked, "Want a ride home?"

My mouth nearly dropped at the sight of his car. It was

a stunning silver Audi A7, and it was the fanciest car I had ever seen in my life. Part of me was afraid that if I breathed too close to it, I would ruin the beautiful metal.

I cleared my throat, trying to fake a nonchalant attitude. I took one last glance at the beautiful car before smiling at him in an attempt at being polite. "Thanks, but like I said yesterday, I prefer to walk home."

"Aww, come on! I could walk you inside, and you could give me a tour."

He looked over me from head to toe once more, with a smirk still curled along his mouth. He didn't even bother trying to hide the fact that his eyes rested on my legs and chest for far longer than they should've. I knew exactly what he wanted a tour of, and it wasn't just my house.

I covered my chest with my arms, trying to hide what his gaze still lingered on. I had brought this on myself though. I never should've worn this ridiculous outfit.

"Maybe some other time. I'll see you tomorrow though."

Before he could object, I spun on my heel and quickly made my way home to change. I was frozen by the time I got there since barely any of my body was covered. After I changed into my normal hoodie and legging attire, I headed out on the route that led to the bookstore.

As I walked through town, I couldn't help but search people's faces for Kaden. I wanted to see a flash of black hair go by or those blue eyes looking towards me. I wanted to feel his strong, secure arms wrap around me to hold me close, but that didn't happen. I didn't see him anywhere, which didn't surprise me. He probably needed his space for now, so he wasn't going to come to places where he knew I would be.

When I was nearly to the bookstore, I looked ahead. There was a short, red headed guy peering into the store through the front window. I didn't know whether to be alarmed by this or apologetic for not having the store opened. I approached cautiously since I didn't know what to make of the situation yet.

"Hi," I said once I had made it over to stand next to him.

He jumped back in surprise and looked at me. His fiery red hair was spiked up in dozens of points, and numerous freckles dotted his pale face. His demeanor shouted anger and hate, and it didn't help that his shirt depicted the devil rising out of burning flames. His dark green eyes bore into me, and he squinted them as if he were trying to figure something out.

"Sorry it took me awhile to get here. I hope you weren't waiting long," I said while unlocking the door.

I stepped inside and allowed him to follow me in. Racing behind the counter, I got things set up in case he made a purchase. When I looked back up, I found him staring at me from across the store. Unbearable silence suddenly wrapped around us, and my blood ran cold. I held my breath as I waited for him to do or say something, but he didn't. He just continued to watch me with narrowed eyes.

My heart began racing the longer that he stood there. I tried piecing together why he wasn't doing anything like looking at the books. I didn't understand why he had been staring into the store if he wasn't even going to look at anything. If he wasn't here for books, the only other thing he could have been waiting for was either me or Mrs. Morea. My skin crawled as his eyes searched me. I swallowed hard as those hungry green eyes told me exactly who he was here for.

My stomach dropped even further, and my fear and anxiety were growing by the minute. He could be the killer in town. He could be the one who'd been attacking me. I didn't recognize him, which was a red flag, because everyone knew each other in this town.

"Are you Raven?" he suddenly asked, his British accent sounding foreign to me.

My skin crawled, and my heart began racing rapidly inside my chest. Not only was he looking for me, but he knew me by name. My throat grew tight at the thought of what he could possibly want with me.

I was frozen to the spot as I stared at him, too afraid to answer. What would happen if I said yes? What would happen if I said no? I didn't know what to do, so I just stood behind the counter, watching him as he watched me. He must've took my silence as the answer he needed though, because he abruptly turned around and walked out.

My knees buckled as the need to vomit overwhelmed me. My mind raced to piece together what the hell had just happened. I let out a shaky breath as I trailed my hand through my hair and shut my eyes. The world was beginning to sway, and I grew dizzy. I fell to my knees, unable to stand any longer. Leaning my back against the counter, I tried to calm down. I had no idea what was going on anymore. So many unanswered questions swam in my head, and it made me feel crushed by the weight of everything.

I forced myself to stand back up, holding onto the counter for support. I sat down on my stool with my head in my hands, and I waited for my anxiety to calm down. For the rest of the night, my eyes would wander to the windows and doors as I waited for the man to come back. I was sure that he was up to no good, and the whole situation made me hope Kaden would show up even more. I knew I was mad at him right then, but I also knew that I felt safe with him. I needed to feel that way right now.

When it was time to close, the same shakiness I'd felt the night I was dragged into the alley and strangled in the Martinezes' basement washed over me. I didn't want to walk home alone in the dark. I wanted Kaden to walk with me the way he had the night I'd babysat, but that wasn't going to happen. He wasn't coming.

I turned off the light to the store then stepped outside. The chill in the air made my heart skip a beat, and I rubbed my arms as I turned to walk home. The vacant streets made it harder to stay calm, as did the approaching alley. It scared me to think that what happened could happen again, but that was reality. There was always going to be danger, and there were always going to be bad people. That was something that I couldn't change, no matter how much I wanted to.

As I stood there, facing the way that led home, I found myself too afraid to move. But suddenly, as I fought with my growing anxiety, I felt a sense of safety. Calm washed over me in a large wave. It was the same sense of comfort I got when Kaden was near. It felt so real, I actually looked around me to see if he was anywhere in sight. My eyes scanned the buildings and searched the shadows, but I failed to find him.

Even so, I faced forward again, the feeling never leaving me. It reminded me so much of his warmth and comfort that I closed my eyes and pretended he was here standing beside me. I smiled softly at the thought of his arm around my waist, like it had been when we'd walked past the alley together that first night.

I opened my eyes again, and thinking of him, my legs took that first step towards home. As I continued walking, I still felt like he was close by. It wasn't just a memory of him being next to me, but rather, it actually felt like he was near me. Anytime I looked around though, he was never there. Even when I thought I caught a whiff of his musky scent in the breeze, he was still nowhere in sight.

Maybe he was following me at a distance, or maybe I was just going nuts. Either way, the thought of him and the promise of his protective words from the night of the fire gave me the strength to walk the rest of the way home with my head held high.

Chapter Eleven

KADEN NEVER SHOWED UP the next day at school. I sat with Simon again, laughing at all his unfunny jokes and pretending to swoon over him. I was getting a bit tired of it, but at least after tonight, I wouldn't have to do it anymore. The date would be done and over with, so I could move on.

"So don't forget," Simon started as we stood by his car after school. "We're meeting at eight in the square."

I gave him a small smile and said, "I know. I'll be there as soon as I'm done at the bookstore."

He smiled and said, "Cool." His eyes traced my tight jeans and barely covered breasts before adding, "Make sure to wear something like this tonight. It looks really good on you." He winked at me, put his sunglasses on, then drove off in his car. I tried not to vomit as I sighed and made my way home.

Simon was going to be in for a rude awakening because I didn't plan on doing anything to impress him tonight. I had faked being into him at school to keep the date on, but the longer I thought about it, the more I wanted this to all be over. I didn't want to go out with him anymore, even if it would make Kaden jealous. I just wanted to find Kaden to figure out what was going on with us.

When I got home, I put on my favorite gray sweater and black leggings. No more dressing up to draw further attention to myself. I was done giving Simon the wrong idea. It was time to end this whole charade.

When I got to the store, I busied myself with shelving books, handling customers, and reading. I did whatever I could to keep myself from dwelling on Kaden or my impending date; however, eight came quickly which meant it was time to close and head to the square. I was putting the money from the cash register into the safe below the counter when the door opened. My heart involuntarily leapt with the hope of it being Kaden, but when I stood back up, it was only Simon.

"Hey," he waved, walking towards the counter.

I gave a half hearted smile and said, "Hey. What are you doing here? I thought we were going to meet in the square?"

He shrugged, leaning against the counter. "I was already out and didn't want to wait, so since I knew where you were, I decided to just meet you here. Are you ready?"

I squatted back down to finish putting the money in the safe. When I was done, I stood back up and grabbed my bag. I nodded to him and said, "Yeah. Let's go."

I stepped around the counter to head to the door, but Simon didn't follow. When I noticed that he wasn't coming,

I turned back around to face him. His questioning gaze followed me, and he wore a deep frown and furrowed brow.

"What?" I asked.

"Aren't you going to change?" He gestured to my sweater and leggings.

"No. This is what I'm wearing. Is there something wrong with that?"

He grimaced and said, "I told you to wear something hot."

I narrowed my eyes at him, disbelieving how big of a jerk he was being. Well, part of me disbelieved his behavior. The other part of me expected nothing less than this attitude.

To be honest, the whole reason I wasn't just telling him off right now was because a big part of me was still hoping to make Kaden jealous. I wasn't a quitter, so since I was already this far into the plan, I was determined to see it through until the end. I could still do that in a sweater and leggings though. I didn't necessarily have to be so exposed.

Looking irritated, he rolled his eyes. He quickly recovered though as he plastered on a smile, and he waved a dismissive hand as he said, "Forget it. I know what you look like under that thing you have on. It can be a surprise for later." He winked at me, and it took everything in me not to outwardly cringe at his words. "Let's just head to the movies."

Together, we walked out of the door, and I had to keep my fists clenched as we did in order to keep myself from slapping him. The condescending ass deserved to be punched. Especially where it would hurt the most.

"So, what movie are we seeing?" I asked as we made it to his parked car. The sight of the beautiful vehicle still sent a wave of awe through me.

"Well," he started, "I don't know if you like horror movies, but there's this new one out that I figured we could see. It's supposed to be super scary, so if you need me to put my arm around you, I will."

He grinned at me from ear to ear, and I stared at him with a raised brow. It took everything in me not to outwardly laugh. I should've known he would try a move like that, but I hadn't expected him to be *so* cliché. How did girls fall for this sort of thing?

"Actually," I began as I slid into the passenger seat. He got in and shut his door, turning his eyes towards me as he started the engine. "I love horror movies."

"Oh," he said. His amusement dwindled slightly. "Well, good."

He pulled out of his parking spot and headed towards the movie theatre. When we got there, he got us a popcorn and Coke to share, but I insisted on having two different straws. I was not putting my lips anywhere near where his lips had been. We went into the showing room for our movie, and he unsurprisingly chose the two seats in the far back right hand corner.

"Now remember," he said, leaning in close, "if you get scared, I'll protect you."

His words made my thoughts immediately go to Kaden, the only person to have ever truly protected me or show me compassion. The thought of him sent my head and emotions on a frenzy again. His bizarre behavior still puzzled me. One minute we were extremely close, and the next, he professed his dislike for me. His behavior the day we'd fought near the woods had cut into me, and it made my head spin in confusion. I wondered if I would ever figure him out and have answers to my questions.

Looking back at Simon with a sarcastic grin, I said, "I'll be fine. I promise."

The lights dimmed, and the previews for the movie began. The whole time, Simon kept talking about how this movie was going to be too much for me and that I needed to prepare myself to be scared. I rolled my eyes at him each time, and I was thankful for the darkness of the theatre so that he couldn't see my reaction.

We sat there with him whispering to me as the previews continued to play. I was starting to wonder if he was ever going to shut up, so when the movie started, I sighed in relief because he finally stopped talking. I was beyond done listening to him go on and on about himself, but I was even more done with him making sexual comments towards me. The only bad part about him not being able to talk was that he took the opportunity to make a move on me.

The story played out on the screen before us, but no matter how hard I tried paying attention, I couldn't focus. Simon kept distracting me. I could see him trying to subtly move his hand closer to my leg, so I crossed them, moving my leg away from his reach. He cleared his throat and tried playing it off like he was just scratching his thigh. I looked at him, and he smiled as he attempted to be cool. I smiled back, but really, I was still wondering how in the world girls fell for this.

We went back to watching the movie. When it got to the part where a girl was about to do the predictable thing by looking under the bed, Simon put his hand on my upper leg. My body stiffened, and I inwardly cringed at his touch. He tried moving his hand over, getting dangerously close to a place he shouldn't, but I quickly grabbed it and placed it back in his own lap. Pulling my feet up into the chair, I hugged my knees to my chest, which worked to protect all of my personal parts.

Looking irritated, he slumped back in his chair with an aggravated huff. He remained that way the rest of the movie while furiously eating popcorn. I guess when he got mad, he took it out on food.

Once the movie was over, I was far too eager to get back to his car. I was more than ready to be separated from him. He still seemed grumpy, but I was okay with that. I didn't care whether or not he liked me. I didn't want to be with him anyways.

We got in the car, and as we pulled out of the theatre I said, "I enjoyed the movie."

He drove with one hand on the steering wheel while resting the other arm on the window to prop his cheek on. He huffed, in a sour mood, and mumbled, "Good for you."

I glared at him, but he didn't notice. "So are you taking me home now?"

"Nope."

He coasted along a road that I had never been down

before, but I knew what it led to: an old farmhouse and barn that all the high schoolers worked on to keep in shape for their various reasons. Each grade used it as a spot to do an array of things like smoke, drink, party, and have sex. As soon as we started going down the deserted road, I knew what Simon had in mind.

With my heart picking up speed, I turned in my seat to look at him. "I'm not doing anything with you Simon. Take me home."

He rolled his eyes. "Chill. It'll be fun. I promise."

"No! I'm not doing a damn thing with you. Let me out, Simon!"

My heart pounded in my chest, and my stomach leapt into my throat. A nervous sweat broke out on my skin. I was starting to realize the dangerous position I had put myself in.

He continued to ignore me with a determined gaze, and panic swelled inside of me. I tried to open the door while he was driving, but it was locked. I screamed at him to unlock the door, and he slammed on the breaks before turning towards me. "Get the hell out then! Go! You can walk home you slut!"

He unlocked the door, so I got out and slammed it shut. Stepping back from the car, I watched as he spun around on the gravel road to head back towards town. Dust and dirt swam around me from his violent driving, and I coughed against its choking hold. I was now left standing alone on the dark, deserted road.

Once his tail lights were gone, the reality of my situation hit me, and a shiver ran up my spine. I slowly peered into the dark woods around me. My palms grew sweaty, and my heart pounded in my ears. I needed to move. I needed to make my legs take me into town, but I was frozen to the spot. Terror filled me to the brim, and my body shook slightly. The surrounding trees blew in the wind, making it sound as if someone was walking towards me.

But the breeze wasn't all I was hearing. I strained my ears and realized what I thought was the wind blowing through the trees was actually footsteps.

And they were headed right for me.

I didn't hesitate as I turned on my heel and started running. My feet crunched against the gravel as my throat dried, and my gasps became raspy. My arms pumped, urging my legs on. I could hear the footsteps behind me. There was more than one set of feet, and they were gaining on me. I pressed harder, closing my eyes as a mix of fear and adrenaline coursed through me. I was crying, sweating, and panting, trying with all my might to run faster.

I was so focused on getting away that I didn't even realize the road had changed back into pavement. My heart stopped as I lost my footing. The tip of my shoe got hung up on the raised edge of the paved road, and time seemed to stop as the ground came up to meet me.

I had been running so fast that I rolled across the road. The rough asphalt scraped across my skin, and the blow of the hard ground sent a sharp jolt through my body. I cried out in pain as I landed hard on my side. A sharp pain encompassed my ankle and the surrounding area, so I knew I'd twisted it. My knees and cheek burned as the cuts on them oozed with warm blood. I looked down at my ripped leggings to evaluate the scrapes on my knees, along with a gash on my right shin. It felt worse than it looked.

I didn't have anymore time to process the pain and what had happened though because before I knew it, a cloth covered my mouth and nose. I struggled at first, tossing my head to the side in an attempt to get away. But the cloth followed me, and after a few dizzy seconds, everything faded to black.

Chapter Twelve

MY EYES SLOWLY FLUTTERED open as soft voices filled the space around me. I blinked, trying to clear the fogginess in my mind. It was dark, and I struggled to know where I was or what had happened.

Shaking my head, my eyes adjusted as small outlines of figures took shape in the darkness before me. I was trying hard to reach out for what had happened when bits and pieces started coming back to me. Simon, the movies, the road, the footsteps. Everything suddenly hit me then at full force. I remembered it all now.

As my mind caught up with what had happened earlier, my current situation was becoming clearer. A wave of sickening panic washed over me as I realized I couldn't move my body. Looking down, I saw itchy, tight ropes binding my arms and legs down to a chair in the middle of an empty room. I whipped my head around to take in the high ceiling, stained glass windows, and raised platform at the head of the room, and I pieced together that I was in an abandoned church. I wasn't alone though.

Standing as a group in front of me were a dozen or so guys. Each wore different expressions, and they were a mix of different races with different features. Some were pasty, others a nice caramel color, and more a beautiful brown. They ranged in size and height, but they all gave off the same terrifying aura. Each of them stared at me with taunting eyes, and I made sure to get a good look at every one of them. I wouldn't go to the cops empty handed this time. That is, if I survived long enough to make it to the cops.

As I continued memorizing features of each of them, I noticed the British guy from the bookstore. I knew he was bad news, but it was too late now. He was standing to the right of someone who looked familiar. The man had black hair with a trimmed beard to match. His dark eyes watched me as he crossed his arms over his broad chest. Trying to clear the rest of the fogginess out of my brain, I shook my head. When I looked back at the man, my heart leapt with hope as I realized who it was.

It was Landon. He would help me!

"I told you that she was still alive," the British guy said. "We should've known that he wouldn't be able to go through with it."

His eyes narrowed in a menacing glare as he looked at me, and fearful tears began to stream down my cheeks. I went to scream, but instead of a shriek coming out, I gagged on a rag that was tied to my mouth. I'd just realized it was there, and a staggering amount of frustration and terror was building up inside of me. With no way to let it out, my head was becoming fuzzy again. My pulse was picking up by the minute, and I was sure I was going to faint again. The fear for my life was becoming overwhelming.

Landon rolled his eyes and shook his head in frustration. "I don't care, Chesed. Just end her. I'll take care of him."

Landon turned to leave, and I squealed and squirmed beyond the rag in my mouth. I couldn't let him walk out and leave me. I didn't understand why wasn't he helping me. And had he just told them to end me? This was Kaden's brother! He couldn't be with these guys.

He turned back around, casting his emotionless brown eyes towards me. I twisted my head in a futile attempt to wrench the rag free from my mouth, and I tried wiggling my body back and forth to break free of the ropes binding me.

"Raven." Landon sighed as he pinched the bridge of his nose in irritation. "Stop struggling. It only makes it worse."

With that, he left. My heart dropped as I realized that he wasn't on my side. He wasn't here to help rescue me. I should've known that as soon as I saw him standing with all of these guys. I was on my own.

As soon as Landon was gone, all the other men surrounded me. They each pulled out a different weapon, ranging from a knife to a gun to a rope. They came closer, laughing and taunting me the more I cried and squirmed. I had to get away. I had to run. I pulled at the ropes as I became surrounded by them, but all it did was cut into my wrists and make them bleed. My heavy breaths and tear drenched face caused a chorus of laughs. They found my efforts amusing.

"Who wants to go first?" a guy with blue hair and purple eyeliner grinned. He licked his lips as if he were hungry before giggling, "I will if no one else wants to."

"No." It was Chesed.

He stepped forward, his knife glinting in the moonlight, reflected through the stained glass windows. I squeezed my eyes shut and wracked painful sobs as I attempted to plead for help, but it was pointless. No one here would help me, and there was no way that I could yell for help.

With the look of a madman, he laughed at my reaction to his knife. He raised it high above his head before bringing it down onto my hip. The feeling of the blade slicing through my skin and into my side burned. I could feel my skin being slit open, as well as the blade plunging deep into my body. It hurt more than anything I had ever felt.

I arched my back in agony and tried kicking my feet as I cried through the cloth that blocked my mouth. Struggling for air, my breathing came out heavy and hard. I could already feel the lukewarm blood dripping down from the wound and onto my thigh.

"Take her muffler off! I wanna hear her scream!" a dark skinned man wielding a wrench shouted.

There was a chorus of agreements as Chesed snickered. With a quick movement of his arm, he sliced the cloth from my face, and it cut my cheek as he did. I gasped for breath while screaming out at the same time. My agonized wails filled the air, and their laughter mixed with the sound. Hot tears streamed down my face, getting into the cut on my cheek. This only made it burn more, causing another moan of torment to escape me.

"Untie her! Let's see her try to fight back!" the guy with the blue hair demanded.

His request was granted as Chesed undid all of my bindings before pulling the chair out from under me. I collapsed onto the cold floor, still crying out in agony. They were all cheering and shoving forward, trying to decide who would get to take their chance at me next. Each of them clawed at me, greedy for their turn. I swatted at them with arms that were growing weaker by the minute.

A bear of a man holding some rope walked up to me as I laid there in a crumpled heap. I was in so much pain by now that I could no longer bring myself to move. Breathing was already becoming difficult too. When they realized that I wasn't fighting back anymore, they all started to boo at me. The man with the rope grew angry, so he kicked me in the side where my cut was. I curled up in pain, letting out another shriek. They laughed, and he took that as encouragement to get on his knees, wrap his rope around my neck, and pull.

I gasped, reaching up to pull at the rope. I kicked my legs in a desperate attempt to do something. I couldn't breathe! He laughed and spat on me, and the other guys joined in all at once. They stabbed me, kicked me, and ripped at my skin and hair.

My vision grew dark and blurry as the pain overwhelmed me and the need to breathe raced through my body. I craved air and the need to be free from the pain. Time was up though. I couldn't breathe anymore, and I prepared myself for the inevitable moment that was about to come. I silently said goodbye to everyone. My dad, Gloria, the Martinezes', Mrs. Morea.

Kaden.

Hs name repeated over and over again in my head as my body shut down. My legs stopped kicking, and my fingers slipped away from the rope around my throat. I reluctantly accepted my fate and stopped struggling when one of the windows to the church suddenly shattered.

The man holding the rope let it go and everyone quickly stood. They looked towards the window as the energy in the room shifted. I sucked in a large amount of air, trying to search through the mass of men standing in front of me to see what had caused the commotion.

I let my head roll to the side, and that's when I saw what they were all looking at. Kaden stood amongst the shattered glass. His body was pulled back in a battle ready stance. My heart soared at the sight of him, and even in the dark, I could see his face scrunched up in utter rage. His shoulders rose and fell, from exertion or anger, I didn't know. All I knew was that I had never seen him so livid.

"Shit," the man with the rope said. Not even a second later, bright orange flames erupted throughout the room, engulfing all of their bodies.

Kaden ran towards me as dozens of agonizing wails escaped from the men around the room. His blue eyes looked down at my broken body, and a mask of utter fear and anguish appeared on his face. Tears were brimming his eyes, and I so desperately wanted to wipe them away. He looked so stricken with grief and worry. I closed my eyes and struggled to open them again. The room was starting to spin, and the ground beneath me seemed to be disappearing. I was fading fast.

He carefully reached down to scoop me into his arms before standing back up. I let my head loll against his shoulder, and that's when I noticed the large black, feathered wings sticking out from his back. I didn't even have time to think before they beat against the air once, raising us up and out of the window he had come in through.

We rose higher into the night air as the pain became unbearable. I looked back into his icy blue eyes one last time before drifting off into a dreamless sleep.

Chapter Thirteen

I GROANED AS I struggled to open my eyes. They felt as though they were glued shut, but I slowly forced them open. It was so dark, with only a small amount of light streaming in from the broken windows. It was night out, so the moon was casting an eerie glow on the wide open room.

I slowly moved my eyes over the place, and I realized I was in an empty warehouse. Well, almost empty. I could feel a fluffy mattress with silk sheets beneath me, and I was covered with a warm, soft comforter.

I wanted to see more of the room, but when I tried lifting up, a jolt of pain shot through my body. I winced before returning to the way I had been lying. My body shook as my vision grew fuzzy at the sides, and I had to gasp for breath.

"I wouldn't move. You're still hurt and recovering."

My heart skipped a beat. Slowly, I looked to my right to see who was there, but there was no need. I knew that voice, and the sound of it made me remember everything that had happened. Panic surged through my body, and I tried lifting up to crawl as far away from him as I could.

Kaden emerged from the shadows to rush to my side. He gently pushed on my shoulders in an attempt to lie me back down. "Stop! I said not to move. Please Raven, just calm down."

"Calm down? Calm down!" I started crying from the pain, confusion, and torn emotions that were coursing through me. "How can I calm down, Kaden? I was nearly killed for the fourth time! Not only that, but now I'm going crazy too! I'm losing my freaking mind."

"You aren't crazy, Raven. Trust me. You're very sane."

I was lying down once more with pain soaring up and down my entire body. The need to vomit was rising up in the pit of my stomach, and I was forced to close my eyes as Kaden sat down next to me. He brushed a strand of my hair back from my forehead as he told me to just breathe in and out slowly until my body stopped hurting. I did as he instructed, and after a few moments, the nausea from the pain subsided.

When the pain lessened, I looked back at him. His dark hair was disheveled as though he had run his hands through it a lot, and his eyes were glassy. My gaze traveled from his eyes to his shoulders. I peeked over them, but I didn't see anything. No wings.

"Where are they?" I asked, gesturing at his shoulder with my chin.

He just stared at me and asked, "Where's what?"

I glared at him. He was avoiding answering me. "You

know what. I saw them, Kaden, so don't try to deny it. You had-" I swallowed hard, still not believing what I had seen. "You had wings. We were flying."

He bowed his head and sighed. "I didn't want you to find out this way."

"Find out what? Find out that you had wings? Please tell me, because the longer I'm left to continue guessing at everything, the crazier I feel."

I closed my eyes and worked to catch my breath after my voice had gotten an edge to it. I was so angry and confused. I was tired of not knowing anything and being left to walk in circles, attempting to figure everything out.

He looked back at me and gave me a half-hearted smile. "You aren't crazy. Everything you saw was real. Including-" he paused, "my wings."

I stared at him with my heart racing. This couldn't possibly be real. I was dreaming. Soon I would wake up and be in my bed at home, and the whole night would be nothing other than a nightmare. There was just no way that this was real. Things like this didn't happen in real life. Guys with wings who could fly! That was just insane! I mean, what did that even make him? A fairy? My mind raced trying to figure all of this out.

I slowly turned to look at him again. He was watching me with those amazing eyes that still had worry buried in them. I let out a shaky breath before daring to ask, "What are you?"

He turned his gaze away from me. I waited for him to start laughing or to tell me that this was all some elaborate joke, but that didn't happen. Instead, he found my eyes again as he slowly said, "I *was* an angel."

My eyes grew wide at his statement. Carefully, I worked to sit up, as the pain was subsiding the longer I was awake. He watched me and chuckled slightly at my amazement. He slid a bit closer to me on the edge of the bed. He still kept his distance from me until he knew how I felt though, which I was thankful for, since I was still trying to figure that part out myself.

"I know," he continued. "It's hard to believe. I probably wouldn't believe it either if I were in your position, but it's true. I was once a high ranking, respected angel. My job was to protect people. I was a guardian angel. I lived every day watching over people and keeping them safe."

He had a far off look on his face as he spoke. He was still looking away from me as he frowned. "But then I broke an angelic law. I fell in love with a human." He glanced at me before looking away again. "She was one of the people I was supposed to be watching over. Falling in love with a human, especially one of my charges, was forbidden, so I was cast out."

I watched him cautiously, and even though it sounded crazy, I felt like he was telling the truth. There was so much remorse and exhaustion in his words and body as he was telling me about who he was. I could tell that he had been struggling with this for some time now.

My heart broke for him as I saw how distraught he was, and hearing his story was difficult. He had lost everything. But if he wasn't an angel anymore, what did that make him?

"So," I began with caution, "What are you? If you're not an angel."

His eyes grew dark, and he spit out his response as though the taste of it repulsed him. "I'm fallen."

He was a fallen angel.

I closed my eyes as my mind raced to piece everything that he had said together. It sounded so crazy, but something inside me insisted that I should believe him. Still needing more answers, I shook my head in confusion. "So are Landon and those other guys fallen angels too?"

He laughed darkly and anger flashed across his previously disgusted expression. "Technically, yes, they are fallen. They were each an angel. Some were cupids, some were messengers, some were counselors. But honestly, I think that they're just as bad as demons now."

"Are demons and fallen angels not the same thing?"

He looked at me, and I realized too late that I may have offended him with that question. I swallowed, hoping I hadn't just said something bad, but he shrugged it off as if it was okay.

He shook his head and said, "No. Demons are fallen angels who have declared their loyalty to Lucifer. Until then, you're just fallen. Someone stuck between two places. That's how Landon and his crew could stand to be in the church two days ago. Demons can't enter any place that is or once was holy, whereas fallen angels can."

I nodded, thinking that made sense when my brain pieced together what he just said. "Wait, did you say two days ago? I've been out for two days?"

All I could think of was work, school, and the duties I had at home that I had missed. Although, that was all starting to sound rather unimportant when compared to what was going on now.

"Calm down," Kaden said in a soothing voice. He scooted even closer to where he could sit directly next to me. Almost as though he could read my mind, he said, "Don't worry about work or school. I've taken care of it. You were hurt really bad." Worry and guilt flooded his face again as he continued. "A two day rest was much needed."

He was right about that. My body was still incredibly sore, and it hurt to just move in the wrong direction or too fast. Luckily, the pain wasn't nearly as bad as it had been the night that it happened.

I nodded and said, "Maybe so, but how did you handle it? What did you do?"

He smiled and said, "One of the things that come with being a guardian angel is the ability to enter someone's dreams. Dreams have a direct link to a person's thoughts, so I simply entered your bosses' dreams and made them believe that they gave you the whole week off. Then to handle the school issue, I've just collected all your work for you and told them that I would take it to you because you were sick and couldn't come."

I smiled, slightly impressed that he had put so much thought into this. He had obviously rescued me that night and taken care of me while I was hurt. On top of that, he'd handled my work and school too.

He was showing me his caring side, which was a side of

him I had really missed recently. Even so, as I started thinking about his words, my smile slowly fell. My mind went back to that night when I dreamt of Kaden coming into my room. He had apologized with no obvious reason, and I wondered if that was a dream after all.

Looking at him with searching eyes, I asked, "Was that you that night? When I dreamt of you coming into my room?"

He gave me a cocky grin and said, "That depends. Have you dreamt of me in your room before? Because if you have, you'll need to be a bit more specific."

I blushed and looked down sheepishly because, truth be told, I had dreamt of him in my room more than just that night. I wasn't going to admit that to him though. If those times had really been him too then he would know for himself how I had dreamt of him. I didn't have to say it out loud.

Still feeling a little warm, I looked back up at him and said, "The dream where you apologized and left without saying anything else. Was that you?"

He continued smiling at me as he leaned in close. His cheek brushed against mine, sending a wave of butterflies through my stomach, as he whispered in my ear, "You didn't deny dreaming of me more than once."

I blushed more before rolling my eyes. "Kaden."

He laughed before leaning back on his hands. When he sat far back enough to look at me, he let his smile fall, and he grew serious. He slowly nodded and said, "Yes. That was me."

Not wanting to meet my eyes, his gaze fell away from mine. He began absently picking at fuzz on the bed that wasn't actually there. He was trying to avoid this conversation, but I wasn't going to let that happen.

"Why did you come to apologize?"

"I was apologizing in advance. The next day was the day-" he stopped, swallowing hard. "-the day that I said those awful things to you. I was hoping that if I told you how sorry I was in your dream, you wouldn't be so hurt when I actually said those things. That of course was a long shot, but I needed to do it. I couldn't bring myself to hurt you like that without trying to at least ease the pain somehow. Although, now that I'm saying it out loud, it doesn't make much sense, huh?"

I didn't know what to say. His words made my mind replay the moment when he'd told me he never wanted to see me again. My chest still constricted when I thought about how cruel he'd been. I looked down at my hands, feeling my eyes grow moist. All the emotions from everything that had happened started piling up inside of me all at once, making it hard to fight against the tears.

"I thought," I sniffed, "I thought that you hated me."

"Never," he said with a flood of tenderness in his tone.

He stood, coming around the bed to the other side. He crawled onto the mattress to where he could lay beside me, and he gently placed his arm around me to pull me closer. It didn't hurt when he held me. It only sent a surge of longing and love through me. I wanted him to hold me in these warm arms forever.

He placed his cheek on the top of my head as he said, "I could never, ever hate you Raven. I can't even tell you how much I regret saying those things. I didn't mean any of it. I thought that if I shoved you away then that would keep you safe from Landon. But I was wrong. He came after you anyways."

I wiped at the tear that had escaped, and I looked at him, noticing how close his face was to mine. If I were to move forward even just slightly, our lips would be touching. Looking up into his eyes, I asked, "Why are they even after me? What do they want?"

He hesitated, staring back into my eyes. He shook his head but didn't break eye contact as he answered, "I don't know."

I swallowed, afraid to ask my next question. "Are they the ones who tried to kill me in the alley and at the Martinezes'?"

He stared at me, and I could tell from how stiff he had grown that he didn't like the answer he was about to give me. "Yes," he whispered.

"Which one was it? Was it Landon?"

He closed his eyes and turned his head away from me. "I don't know which one it was."

After a few moments, his gaze returned to mine. We continued staring into each others eyes, and despite the news of Kaden being a fallen angel and there being bad guys out to kill me, I actually felt a tiny bit of relief. I had gotten some answers that explained a lot of Kaden's bizarre behavior, as well as a little information that explained the attacks on me.

I no longer felt so in the dark about everything going on around me. Even if I didn't have all the answers, maybe we could find them together.

I was seeing Kaden in a better light, and even though his story was still crazy, I believed him one hundred percent. I had seen his wings with my own eyes. I had felt the wind kiss my skin as he flew. I knew this was real. He was real. His warm arms around me, his blue eyes looking into mine, his body close to me. This was all real, and the longer he looked at me like that, the more my heart went crazy. It was pounding so hard that I was positive he could hear it.

He gently brought his hand up to brush a strand of my hair back before letting it pause on my cheek. I closed my eyes, pushing my cheek further into his hand. It felt strong and safe. These hands would protect me.

I opened my eyes to look back at him, and he started to lean in closer. I closed my eyes, preparing myself for his kiss, but he stopped short. He cleared his throat and slowly moved to get off the bed.

"I think that I'm going to go up to the roof to fly around," he said as he stood up. His eyes met mine again, taking in my disappointed expression. He gave me a small smile as he added, "Night is really the only time I can stretch my wings out and fly. You should rest some more anyways."

Looking away from him, I nodded. Color spread across my cheeks as I grew embarrassed by the fact that we'd nearly kissed. I'd been going along with it in the heat of the moment, but now that I was left to think about it, my nerves were on fire. Even so, I was a bit disappointed by the fact that he'd stopped.

"Yeah, go for it," I said.

I looked down to avoid his gaze, and I realized for the first time that my clothes had been changed. I was wearing a large white t-shirt and sweatpants that must have been Kaden's.

"Where are my clothes? When did I get in these?"

He grinned from ear to ear before saying, "The clothes you had on were cut up and stained with blood, so I changed you into some of my clothes."

My cheeks grew fiery hot, and my eyes grew wide at the thought of Kaden undressing me. He laughed at my reaction and turned to head up the steps that lead to the roof. "Don't worry. I didn't look." The heat on my cheeks began to subside, and I let out a small sigh of relief before he glanced over his shoulder and added, "Much." He snickered then made his way up the rest of the stairs.

Still blushing, I sat there for a few moments. I decided to lay back down and process everything that Kaden had just told me. He wasn't human; he was a fallen angel who could fly, enter dreams, and who knew what else. It was nice to think that he was protecting me and cared about me, but I felt somewhat confused too.

Kaden had fallen in love with someone else, some other girl. I didn't understand why he was here with me and not with her. It occurred to me that maybe something had happened to her, which was why Kaden was with me and not her anymore. I also began to worry about the possibility of him still loving her. He obviously cared about me or else he wouldn't have saved me and taken care of me the way he had, but what if he still longed for her too?

Falling in love is a big deal. To me, a person only falls in love once, so there was no way that he could just be over her, especially if he literally *fell* for her. I didn't know if it was silly of me to feel slightly jealous over the situation, but I did. I didn't want to potentially lose Kaden if he still had feelings for this other girl and she showed up.

How could I compete with the girl he fell in love with?

Chapter Fourteen

I TOSSED AND TURNED as I tried forcing myself to go to sleep, but I couldn't. I had too much on my mind, so I slowly sat back up, pushing the covers aside. I took a deep breath before sliding to the edge of the bed. A sharp pain erupted along my side as I stood up, but I just paused, letting the pain fade. When I was sure I was fine and able to walk, I slowly made my way further into the room.

I approached the stairs that were to my left. Making my ascent carefully, it became evident that the upstairs loft was empty just like the main part of the warehouse. The only thing in the room was a ladder nailed into the wall that led to the rooftop. Kaden didn't seem to have very many possessions, which made me curious about the kinds of things he did covet.

My feet dragged across the cold floor as I walked to the ladder. Taking in a deep, steadying breath, I reached for one of the rungs and tried to take a step up. The attempt to pull myself up sent a terrible pain up my side where Chesed had stabbed me. I winced and grabbed at my side as I dropped back down to my feet. I gritted my teeth and clenched my eyes shut as I waited for the pain to go away. My breathing became ragged, and the jolt of pain was making my head fuzzy.

I was forced to slump against the wall as the urge to vomit overtook me. I tried calming my breathing as I looked up through the opening in the roof, and I searched for any sign of Kaden. My ears strained to catch any sort of sound, and relief flooded me when I heard the gentle flap of his wings hitting the air. He was keeping close to the roof.

"Kaden," I called, cupping my hand around my mouth. I waited and listened as the sound of his wings got even closer to the opening. The echo of feathers hitting air stopped as he landed, and after a moment, he came into view, looking down at me through the hole.

"What are you doing up?" he asked with a hint of alarm. He jumped down through the door and landed gracefully in front of me.

His brow was pulled forward and his mouth turned down in a worried frown. I could hardly focus on his face though because he was standing there without a shirt. His body was built perfectly, looking every bit as amazing as I'd figured it would. The muscles on his arms, chest, and stomach were sculpted, and his skin was flawlessly colored in a beautifully tanned peach. It left me breathless and blushing.

I quickly averted my eyes back to his before he caught me staring any longer than I had been. Luckily, he wasn't focused on the fact that I had been staring at his half-naked body. Instead, he crouched down to where we were face to face as his hands roamed all over me, checking to see if I had hurt myself any further.

"How did you get up here?"

"I can walk," I said with an easy laugh. "But when I tried climbing the ladder, I couldn't. That *did* hurt." I grabbed my side again as if to show him what I meant, but he didn't need clarification.

He shook his head at me and questioned, "Why are you up here? Why were you trying to climb the ladder?"

I shrugged. "I couldn't sleep, so I came up here to watch you fly. I didn't really get a chance to see it well before."

Shaking his head once more, he smiled and closed his eyes. Still grinning at me, he pulled me to him and said, "Hold on then."

A smile spread across my lips. I wrapped my arms around his neck as he scooped me up gently, cradling me to his warm body. His dark wings sprang out once more with a loud smack, lifting us up through the hole and out into the air. My heart caught in my throat as he lifted us up into the clouds.

The air was cool and relaxing as it surrounded me. The only source of light was the moon and stars, but I felt so close to them that it was more than enough to light up the midnight sky. I closed my eyes, smiling at the wondrous feeling of soaring high. The sky was marvelous with all its close up beauty. Kaden glided smoothly through it, watching me with a smile.

His shiny, black wings stroked us forward towards a

cloud. I reached out and grabbed at it. It was so cool against my broken body, and even though it disappeared as soon as my hands met it, it was the lightest and softest thing that I had ever touched. I tilted my face up as he continued to fly, letting my hair dance in the wind. I couldn't stop grinning. Never had I felt so free and alive. Flying like this with Kaden, I didn't have a care in the world.

"This is beautiful," I whispered, looking around once again. I felt his arms tighten around me, and my smile deepened at the touch.

We circled back over Kaden's warehouse before coming down to land. My legs felt like jelly after being in the air, and he had to hold me up once he let me back on my own feet. After a few moments though, we both sat down, still staring at each other.

"That was incredible!" I was still so mesmerized. I looked at his wings, which were still spread out behind him. They were so beautiful, spanning just a bit longer than Kaden's arm length. They were the deepest black that I had ever seen, yet they somehow still had a luminosity to them.

"Your wings are incredible too," I said breathlessly. My cheeks flushed as they always did when I was around him. "I don't think I've ever seen something more stunning."

The smile that he had worn while we were flying slowly disappeared. He looked at each wing over his shoulders and shook his head sadly. "They aren't stunning. They used to be though. When I was still an angel, they were this amazing white. Even whiter than the purest, most freshly fallen layer of snow on the ground. These-" he paused, looking at each wing, "these are a curse. They're dark like the person I've become. All they do is remind me that I'm no longer an angel."

I sat there in silence, not knowing what to say. The amount of pain in his voice was hard to hear. I didn't know what it was like to go from an angel to fallen, but what I did know was that Kaden wasn't dark. He was still good and wonderful, inside and out.

For a moment, all I could do was look at him. He was staring at the ground with a look that was stricken with grief. His eyes weren't shining like normal, and his pink lips were turned down at the corners. Finally, I scooted closer, closing almost all of the space between us.

"They don't seem like a curse to me. I think they're gorgeous, and if it hadn't been for what you find to be a curse or punishment, I never would have gotten to meet you. We wouldn't be here together if it was different, because you would still be out in the world guarding people. To me, these," I said, gesturing to his wings, "are a blessing because I was able to meet you and find a friend in you."

I met his eyes once more as he stared deeply into mine. Our gazes became lost within each others', and at first, I couldn't read his expression. Before I knew it though, his wings wrapped around me, encasing me in their soft touch. They pulled me all the way to him, and he reached out to gently grab my waist. He was careful to avoid my injuries as he brought me closer, until I straddled his lap. My heart thudded against his bare chest.

He watched me as I decided to take the opportunity to

slowly reach my hand out to touch his wing. It was even softer and silkier than a normal bird's feather. These felt lighter, like the softest silk in the world. I smiled and laughed under my breath as I admired how incredible they felt passing in between my fingers.

I moved my hands along them, until I came to the end where my hands moved onto his shoulders then up his neck and into his hair. I tangled my fingers into his soft, black waves as he leaned forward, pressing his lips against mine. His arms encircled me, trying to draw me nearer even though there was no space left between us.

He kissed me passionately, opening my lips slightly with his. His kiss seemed urgent, as if he had been waiting for this for a long time. It left my heart fluttering as he opened my lips even further to let his tongue reach for mine. I tugged at his hair in an attempt to bring him closer. I wanted to feel more of him.

He moved away from my mouth and kissed on my jawline. His soft lips traced down my neck, which sent a shiver through me. His body responded to this, as he raised up to gently guide me to the rooftop, where he laid me on my back. His lips found mine again as his hands moved down my sides and onto my hips. Resting his body in between my legs, I felt nerves crash through my body at our position. I didn't care though. I wanted Kaden.

He pulled back slightly, panting from kissing without pause. His eyes remained closed as he rested his forehead against mine. My fingers were still in his hair, and his arms were still circled around me as he continued to hover above me. I didn't want him to stop. I wanted to keep going until there was nothing between us.

His blue eyes stared into mine for a moment, most likely deciding what to do next. I waited with nervous anticipation for his next move. He let out another heavy breath as he stood, picking me up with him. Walking over to the opening in the roof, he lowered us both down it. Still carrying me, he walked down the stairs into the main room. He approached the bed and gently placed me back on the soft mattress. I watched him as I waited for him to say something, anything. My nerves were electrified after kissing, and the silence wasn't helping.

He gave me a soft smile as he whispered, "Goodnight, Raven."

He turned and went back up the stairs. I stared at the place he had been standing as a mix of embarrassment and warmth spread across my skin. That kiss had been so passionate, I almost didn't know what to do with myself. But it had also ended as soon as it started. Kaden's reaction afterwards was also not what I was expecting.

I didn't have time to think about it anymore though. As soon as my head found the pillow, my eyelids drifted shut, and sleep pulled me deep under its spell.

Chapter Fifteen

LIGHT SHONE THROUGH THE broken windows of Kaden's warehouse. The warmth that radiated from its rays covered my body as my eyes fluttered open. Forcing myself awake, I tried blinking away the rest of the sleep that was calling my name. Remembering I was in Kaden's bed, I rolled over onto my side, expecting to come face to face with him. After all, it was his bed, and since things seemed to be progressing between us, it only made sense that he would be in bed with me. But when I rolled over, I was greeted by an empty spot. He wasn't there.

I gradually sat up as I looked around for him. Glancing down to my right, I found him lying on the floor, covered with a large throw blanket and small pillow. I smiled, finding it very sweet that he had slept on the floor, but at the same time, a huge wave of guilt hit me. I hadn't meant to put him out of his own bed.

I slowly pushed the blankets aside as I eased out of the bed. He was right next to it, still sleeping soundly. Not wanting to wake him, I carefully put one leg out to step over him, but when I got to the point where I was straddling him, he suddenly reached out to grab my waist. He gently pulled me down on top of him with a wide grin. He kissed me softly, and a sweet pulse of heat bounced around in my chest. When he looked at me again, his eyes had a bright shine to them, and his smile matched.

"Good morning to you too," I giggled.

Still holding me on his lap, he sat up, and not once did he stop smiling at me. "How do you feel this morning?"

"Much better," I said, wrapping my arms around his neck.

It was true. I felt much better. The sleep had helped tremendously. Granted, my side still ached when I moved a certain way, but I really felt like I was in better shape than the previous night. Sore but alive.

He happily nodded as he kissed my neck once, and the gesture still made my heart flutter. His eyes found mine again as he got a playful grin on his face. He knew exactly what his kisses did to me. I leaned down until our lips met, pulling his body closer to mine. He wrapped his arms around me, and in one swift motion, he rolled over until he was on top of me. My cheeks warmed, and he laughed at my response to him.

He kissed me once more on the forehead before jumping to his feet. Smiling down at me, he asked, "Are you hungry?"

I couldn't help but feel slightly disappointed. He had pushed me away again. Granted, I felt a bit nervous about kissing and being so close, but at the same time, I couldn't help but be drawn to the satisfying electric spark it drew up inside of me. There was so much between us, especially now that I knew his secret. I couldn't explain the tie that bound us together, but it was there. I craved to know more of him, and my body yearned for his warm touch.

I didn't have much time to think about his abrupt stop though, because as soon as my brain registered the word *hungry*, my stomach let out a deep growl. I was starving! I hadn't eaten in three days!

"I'm insanely hungry," I admitted.

He reached his hand out to me, helping me up to my feet. "Let's get you something to eat then."

He went over to a pile of clothes on the floor and picked up what appeared to be one of my sweaters and a pair of jeans. I raised my eyebrow in question, and he smiled, saying, "I may or may not have gone into your house in the middle of the night to get you some clothes. I figured you would be more comfortable in your own stuff."

His eyes took all of me in from head to toe, admiring his own baggy clothes on my small frame. He gave me a mischievous grin and added, "Although, if you wanted to stay in my clothes, I wouldn't mind. It's pretty sexy."

I smiled sheepishly as I reached out to take my clothes from him. Looking back into his eyes, I asked, "How did you get in?"

"I'm a fallen angel, remember?" he smirked. "I have my ways."

I shook my head and rolled my eyes as he laughed. He

pointed at a door to my right and said, "That's the bathroom. There's a tub and an overhead shower if you want to wash up."

I smiled and nodded. "Thank you."

I carried my clothes with me as I walked into the tiny room. It was only big enough to house the sink, toilet, and tub, which had an overhanging shower head attached to it. I looked back out at Kaden, who watched me with a smile as I shut the bathroom door.

I released the breath I had been holding as I turned on the hot water to the shower. As I laid my clothes down and let the water heat up, I attempted to tug Kaden's shirt off, but I stopped short. Each time I lifted my right arm, a sharp pain shot up through my entire body. Even though I was feeling better, my side wasn't ready to stretch in that direction. I winced, and my breath became heavy every time I tried to stretch my arm up. The waves of pain it sent through my body were still making me dizzy.

I leaned against the wall, trying to calm my breathing and stop the jolts of painful electricity running through me. I knew I wasn't going to be able to get this shirt off by myself, but the thought of Kaden helping me take it off made me feel even dizzier than what the pain was causing. Then again, he had already changed me once, so if he helped me again, it wasn't like it would be any different.

I let out a nervous breath as I slowly peeked out of the bathroom door. Kaden was halfway through changing himself. He was shirtless and had just finished tugging on a pair of pants when he realized I had opened the door. His blue eyes looked through his black strands of hair that had fallen across his face, and the corners of his lips turned up slightly. My eyes grew wide, and my cheeks heated with embarrassment.

I quickly ducked my head and said, "I'm sorry. I didn't realize that you were changing."

His gentle laugh surrounded my entire being as he walked over to me. He put his finger under my chin and tilted my face up to look into his eyes. I could see out of my peripheral vision that he was still shirtless though, which didn't help to calm my nerves.

I swallowed hard as he smiled at me. "It's okay. Did you need something?"

"I- I can't..." I stammered, having trouble forming the words.

"You can't what?" He let his hand rub up and down my arm in an attempt to soothe me.

His efforts obviously worked because I finished, "I can't get my shirt off."

He looked down at my body, trying to hide his grin. "Oh." He cleared his throat, unable to keep his smile at bay. "Well that's an easy fix."

He gently pushed me back into the bathroom, and he lifted my shirt at the bottom, looking at my stab wound. I dared to peek at it too, and I was surprised to see black thread holding the red skin together.

Glancing up at him, I asked, "Did you stitch this?"

He nodded. "The night I brought you here, you were losing too much blood. I've had my fair share of experiences with stitching, so I used the time while you were unconscious to do it."

"Wow," I mumbled. Looking back down at the stitched slice in my skin, I outwardly shivered. Dried blood covered the slit, and the sight of it made me grow nauseous. I hated the sight of blood, so I was glad I'd stayed unconscious while he stitched me up.

He looked back into my eyes and asked, "You can't lift your right arm or else it hurts, right?"

I nodded. He looked back down at my shirt before carefully lifting up the left side of the fabric. He lifted my left arm and pulled it through the sleeve, exposing the left side of my upper body. I held my breath, as part of me was afraid I would pass out from all the butterflies coursing through me. He tugged the shirt over my head, while leaving my right arm still in the sleeve. He gently shrugged it off down the length of my right arm, and not once was I forced to raise it up. He made it look incredibly easy, and I was happy to report it was painless.

My relief quickly turned into embarrassment, however. I slowly crossed my arms over my chest as my color deepened. I was only standing in my bra and pants now, which was sending my nerves into a frenzy. He took a step forward to press his body against mine, pinning me against him and the sink. I glanced back at him to find his eyes roaming all over my bare skin, with an adoring smile playing at his lips. I swallowed hard as his finger traced over my shoulder and down the length of my bra strap.

He slid it from my shoulder as he looked into my eyes.

Learning forward slightly, he asked, "Do you need help with anything else?"

His finger moved from my fallen bra strap over the top of my chest, and down the line in between my breasts. I let out a ragged breath as his fingertips electrified my skin, and the noise seemed to spark a fire in his eyes.

Embarrassed by the sound I had just made, I bit my lip. I quickly turned away from him, shaking my head to let him know that I was okay. I peeked at him through the corner of my eye, my cheeks flushed. The corners of his mouth turned down slightly as he watched me, and disappointment was embedded in his eyes.

He took a step back and gave me a small smile. "Well, if you need anything else, just let me know."

I nodded as he turned to walk out of the bathroom, shutting the door behind him. Frozen, I stood there for another moment, unable to believe what just happened. My heart raced from the emotions that his roaming fingers had brought on, and I couldn't shake the image of him half naked out of my mind.

When I finally calmed down and my head was clear again, I stepped into the shower. I stood there, letting the water wash away the lingering sensations his touch had brought on. My skin was on fire in a really good way, and my heart was beating erratically in my chest. I was incredibly thrilled and excited by these emotions, but still, I needed to clear my head.

I finished washing, and once the water became cold, I climbed out of the shower. I pulled my pants and bra back on then carefully attempted what Kaden had done to get my shirt off, only I did it in reverse to put it on. When I'd finished getting dressed and drying my hair, I took slow steps out of the bathroom. I was nervous to meet his eyes again.

Kaden was lying back on his elbows, facing the bathroom. His blue eyes traced every inch of me as a smirk formed on his lips. I gulped. My eyes roamed his body as I took in how incredibly good he looked in his dark clothing. The intimacy of how it had felt when he was in the bathroom with me flashed back to my mind. As I remembered the moment, a heat spread across my cheeks and ears, and I was forced to look away from him.

He stood, and I looked sideways at him as he asked, "Are you ready to go?" I gave him a grin and nodded. He smiled sweetly at me and said, "Good. Let's go then."

We made our way outside, and at first, Kaden offered to carry me or help me to walk. It made me happy that he was still worried about me, but at the same time, I felt perfectly fine walking. Only after my insisting multiple times that I was comfortable walking on my own did we make our way towards town, hand in hand.

We followed the line of trees along the road, hiding within its deep shadows. Kaden's gaze continued to dart all around us as he searched near and above us for any sign of Landon or his goons.

I looked around us too, peering into the naked trees on my right. My eyes searched in between their dark silhouettes, attempting to catch any glimpse of a passing shadow or hiding figure. I don't know if it was Kaden's presence or the fact that I didn't sense anything around us, but for some reason, I wasn't the least bit afraid.

I turned my attention back towards Kaden, who was staring past me into the woods, his eyes still searching. "Do they know where you live?"

He blinked and looked at me. "Huh?"

"Landon, Chesed, all of them. Do they know where you live?"

He shook his head. "No. I broke off from them to be by myself, and I never let them follow me home or find out where I was staying. I liked my personal space."

"Then why are you looking around like something is going to jump out and get you?" I gave a small laugh.

He smiled and shrugged his shoulders. "Habit, I guess. Always looking to keep people safe."

I smiled warmly at him. With the way he made me feel secure and protected, I knew he must have been an excellent guardian angel. I wondered if my guardian angel was watching me right now, seeing me walking side by side with a fallen angel. What a sight that must be! I looked around once more into the trees, but I wasn't searching for Landon or his men this time. Instead, I was trying to see if I could spot my own guardian angel.

"What are you looking for?" he asked, nudging me gently with his elbow.

I looked back at him and asked, "Did you know my guardian angel? Are they here right now?"

He furrowed his brow and looked at the ground. Kicking a rock, he stared across the road away from me. I watched him as he slowly nodded and said, "Yeah. I knew him. He- he's here. Sorta." He looked back at the ground before closing his eyes and shaking his head. "Let's talk about something else. I probably don't need to be talking about your guardian angel."

Feeling tension growing, I looked away from him. He was obviously very against talking about this. Maybe Kaden and my guardian didn't get along, or maybe there was some sort of rule that prevented him from talking about it, even as a fallen angel. That would explain his behavior when I tried asking him about it. Still, it didn't stop my mind from wandering.

I reluctantly decided to drop the subject in order to talk about something else. Now was a good time to ask more questions that would help me to better understand everything, so meeting Kaden's eyes once more, I said, "You don't seem anything like Landon or those guys. I mean you never hurt me like they did, so why were you with them?"

He sighed and said, "It wasn't necessarily by choice." He stepped to the side, pulling us further into the trees. I guess he didn't want to take any chances of someone seeing us.

"When I fell, they were there as soon as I woke up. Fallen angels have this sort of sixth sense that lets them know when a new fallen angel is being cast out. There are groups like Landon's everywhere, spread throughout the globe. It just so happened that he was the one nearby when I landed. Groups like his seek out as many fallen angels as they can because the more you have in your group, the more pain and damage you can cause."

My mouth dropped open. "That's awful! Why do they want to hurt so many people?"

"They're all angry." He stopped walking, and he turned to look directly in my eyes. "All of them are furious with Heaven and the Father for making them fallen. All they can think of is getting revenge on Him, and they do so by hurting or killing humans, His most precious children. They carefully select certain targets and plot out the perfect way to end them."

"Is that why they are after me?"

He took in a sharp breath and held it as he hesitated. His body visibly froze, and I waited with anticipation for his answer. That moment never came though. His cool eyes searched mine for another moment before he turned and continued walking towards town. He had avoided my question, which was strange. Now that all his secrets were out and he could be open, he had nothing more to hide. So why couldn't he answer me?

In fact, now that I thought about it, anytime I'd asked him why they'd come after me, he'd seemed to falter and pause. I was beginning to think that he knew more than he was letting on, but was it so bad that he felt like he couldn't tell me? What reason could have him too afraid to confide in me?

I was just about to ask him about this when he continued our earlier conversation. "So Landon and the boys found me and welcomed me in. When I decided that I didn't like what they were doing and wanted out, I left the group, which left them a lot less powerful."

"Why did you leaving make them less powerful? I thought it was all about how many you had in the group. One less angel doesn't seem that drastic."

He shook his head. "Numbers is a big part of it, but what really makes the group powerful is having someone who was a guardian angel in the group. Guardians have a special ability that other angels don't. We use it to protect our charges. If a group can get a guardian on their side, they can utilize that power to the group's advantage."

"You have a power!" I grabbed onto his arm and smiled way too big, but he laughed, not seeming to mind.

"Yeah. I do."

"What is it?"

"Take a wild guess," he grinned.

My mind traced back to all the times that I had seen Kaden, and I worked to piece together if I could recall him doing anything out of the ordinary. Granted, his behavior had always been abnormal, but I knew that wasn't what he was talking about. The dream situation was definitely different, but he had already said that a lot of angels had that ability. This had to be something more specific, something guardians could use as a sort of defense to protect their charges.

The other night when he saved me from Chesed and those other angels came to mind. When he showed up, everyone seemed to panic before going up in flames without any cause. Or at least, at the time there had not seemed to be a cause.

Looking at him with a proud and confident smile, I declared, "Fire! That's your power."

He grinned and kissed my forehead as we continued walking once more. "Good girl. You got it. My power is fire. Granted, it's not what it used to be, but at least I still have the ability. When I was angelic, I could create this pure, white fire just by sheer will."

His smile faded and something dark crossed his features. "Now I can only create simple, ordinary fire. I can't even will it anymore. I have to open and close my fists to create it while focusing on a target, and setting more than one thing on fire at the same time like I did in the church that night takes a lot out of me now."

His usual carefree features were scrunched up in a troubled expression, and I hated seeing him that way. I searched my mind for something that I could say to cheer him up. Slowly, I tried, "Ordinary fire, huh? You think being able to produce fire is ordinary? White flame or not, that's still pretty awesome. Ordinary definitely isn't the right word. Extraordinary is a much better term."

He smiled at me, and I was happy to see it was a genuine smile. My words had cheered him up. He was finally smiling that sexy grin that seemed to make my heart beat faster. He was far too hard on himself for being a fallen angel. Why couldn't he see the amazing person that I saw when I looked at him?

"Thank you," he said, still smiling. "That means a lot to me."

I smiled back at him. "Well, it's the truth." I let my

smile fall as I began to chew the inside of my lip. "So, they aren't as powerful now because they don't have your power on their side." I said it more as a statement than as a question, but he nodded to let me know that I was on the right track. "Does anyone else in the group have powers like you?"

He shook his head. "No. Just me. None of the others guys were guardian angels before they fell, so none of them have my special abilities. To inflict any damage, they have to use actual weapons, just like a human."

I thought back to that night they'd attacked me. They'd all used weapons of some kind. There had been nothing supernatural about that night until Kaden showed up. His words made sense when I thought about everything. The only thing that I still didn't understand was why they were after me, but I wasn't going to ask again. He had already explained that it was probably because they were just trying to get revenge on God.

My eyes traveled back to Kaden as it occurred to me that he really did have a good heart. He was so much different than the other fallen angels, and even though him being fallen was supposed to mean he was evil, he was far from it. I wasn't sure if it was just the guardian instincts still embedded in him or if it was something else entirely. Either way, Kaden was no monster.

It also dawned on me just how powerful he was. That was obvious, not only by the fact that he was once a guardian, but even the other fallen angels acknowledged his power and abilities. They feared him, and it was as if they knew they were going to be done for when he came to save me.

"If you were the most powerful, why didn't you fight to be the leader of the group? Why is Landon in charge?"

"I wouldn't want to lead them in their pursuit to hurt innocent people. Landon is in charge because he was the first to fall in that particular group. He has the most experience as a fallen angel, and the others respect and fear him because of that."

I kicked a rock and worked to soak in all he was saying. Was I insane for believing Kaden and trusting him so easily? Probably. But it was either trust his word or admit I was insane, and that was something I wasn't ready to do.

Pushing my thoughts away, I glanced at him as I said, "Well, it sucks for Landon because he just lost a whole lot of his men the other night when you set them all on fire."

I watched him as he shook his head sadly. "They likely didn't die, Raven. The most it did was probably burn them a bit. That's another downside to this fire that I have now. It's so weak when I do a lot of it at one time. I guarantee you that the flames only lasted a few seconds after we escaped."

"Oh," I said, matching his disappointed expression. I swallowed and asked, "So they are still out there then?"

He stopped walking and turned me to look at him. I gazed into his familiar, loving eyes as he pulled me closer to place a soft kiss on my lips. When he pulled back, he cupped my cheeks in his warm hands as he said in his reassuring, husky voice, "I will never let anything happen to you again."

A smile spread across my lips, and I leaned forward to kiss him. His lips were eager to meet mine, and the kiss quickly intensified. He plunged his hands into my hair as he pushed me back slightly to pin me against a tree. I tugged at his shirt, pulling him closer as my heart soared. He shoved my lips apart with his, begging for more of me. His hands moved down from my hair and onto my waist, pushing me further back against the tree, even though there was no room for me to move back anymore.

His body pressed hard against mine, and his hand scooted further down onto my hip. That's when he accidentally squeezed the place where I was stabbed. Pain ricocheted through me as I pulled back to let out an agonizing wail. Kaden stepped away quickly, realizing too late what he had done. I clenched my eyes shut, and I collapsed to my knees as a wave of nausea flowed through me. Kaden hurriedly grabbed me before I could hit the ground all the way, and he pulled me onto his lap.

"Raven, I'm so sorry! I wasn't thinking!"

I tried to slow my erratic breathing, but I had to quickly shove away from him and lean behind the tree as I threw up stomach acid. I heaved as Kaden slowly crawled closer to pull my hair away from my face and rub small circles on my back. I remained there on my knees, holding myself up with arms that were quickly growing weak. I had nothing in my stomach, and being forced to vomit despite that stripped every bit of energy I did have.

After I knew I was done vomiting what little substance I had in my stomach, I leaned back against the tree and wiped my mouth with the back of my hand. My head was spinning, so I kept my eyes closed for a moment in order to collect myself. I breathed in the cool air, allowing it to soothe me.

When I was sure I was composed enough to see straight, I glanced at Kaden. His mouth and eyes were turned down as a deep look of guilt and worry washed over him.

I shook my head and swallowed. "It's okay, Kaden. It wasn't your fault. You forgot. We both did."

"It was my fault," he said bitterly. "I should've been thinking more clearly." He closed his eyes and angrily ran his hands through his hair. "I can't keep a straight head when I'm around you like that."

I placed my hand on his arm. "No, Kaden. I should've been the one being more careful. It's not your fault. Please, don't feel bad about this. I probably just need to eat something. I'm sure that would make me feel a lot better."

He reluctantly nodded before standing. He leaned down to help me to my feet, but my knees buckled. He quickly wrapped one arm around my waist, while using the other to bring my arm up and around his shoulders. I was more than happy to feel his strong, secure arms around me as I still felt slightly off. We stayed like that as we made the rest of the way into town together.

Chapter Sixteen

S SOON AS WE got to the small bakery, the warmth kissed me all over, and the smell of bagels swam around me. I smiled softly, and my stomach let out a ferocious growl. Kaden laughed softly, shaking his head.

He led me to a booth against the sidewall, where he helped me to sit down. He got in line to order us two bagels with cream cheese and coffees. When he came back and sat my bagel in front of me, he barely had time to sit down before I was biting into the toasted bread. I didn't even bother to take the time to relish the taste. I just wanted to eat! I hadn't realized how hungry I was.

Laughing, Kaden said, "Poor girl. I starved you."

I swallowed my mouth full before looking up at him. "I was asleep. That wasn't your fault."

He continued to smile at me as he sipped his coffee. I ate my bagel in no time, and my stomach continued to growl, so he went and bought me another one. I watched him as he waited in line once more. His back was to me, but

I still gazed after him with a grin plastered on my face.

I wasn't sure what I'd done to deserve someone as amazing as him. As I spent more time with Kaden, I noticed how much he had changed. At first I was sure he was nothing but trouble and a guarantee for heartbreak, but it was clear to me now that his behavior at the beginning of our relationship was just a facade. In reality, he was incredibly caring and thoughtful, and I was at my happiest when I was with him. No one had ever cherished me the way he seemed to. He was everything I had been dreaming of and more. I really did care about him, even if we had only known each other for a few months.

I watched him as he ducked his head down and tiredly rubbed at the back of his neck. This motion caused the neck of his shirt to come down in the back, exposing the hint of what looked to be some sort of tattoo. He was too far away though, and I couldn't quite make out the details. When he returned, he wore a killer smile as he handed me my second bagel.

I took a big bite to settle my demanding stomach, and after swallowing, I asked, "What's your tattoo of?"

He involuntarily rubbed at the back of his neck as he quirked his eyebrow. "How did you know about my tattoo?"

"I saw it when you were standing in line. What's it of?"

He smiled more broadly at me and said, "It's actually not a tattoo. It's a marking. Almost all angels have one on their back. It signifies what animal or element of nature they can shapeshift into."

My eyes grew wide as I struggled to swallow the bite I

had just taken out of my bagel. "You can shapeshift?"

He nodded, still grinning from ear to ear.

"The things I keep learning today," I mumbled under my breath. He heard me though because he let out a sweet, smooth laugh that made my heart catch slightly. My eyes found his once more as I smiled at him and asked, "So what do you transform into? Is yours an animal or something like a tree?"

"A tree?" He quirked his eyebrow again, laughing slightly.

I shrugged my shoulders. "Trees are nature."

He shook his head, never ceasing to smile. "It's not a tree."

"Tell me what it is!" I said, matching his grin.

I had finished my bagel, so now all my focus was on him. Before he could answer me though, two Barbie dolls from my school approached our table. My stomach dropped as I watched them saunter towards us. I was positive they were here for Kaden, but to my astonishment, I found their smiles and gazes directed towards me.

"Hey Raven," the girl with a pink sundress said.

It was Lily. She was the head of both the swim team and dance team. Why she was wearing a sundress in October was beyond me. Then again, I had worn even less clothing when I was attempting to make Kaden jealous, so I really had no room to talk.

"Uh," I stuttered. I wasn't too sure what to do, so I just quirked my eyebrow slightly at her. "Hey?" I didn't mean for it to come out sounding like a question, but I wasn't able to hide my bewilderment. I was at a loss for words.

"We heard about you going out with Simon the other night!" the other one said. She was wearing even less clothing than Lily. Ms. No Clothes was Brittany, head of the cheer team.

"Yeah. That's, like, totally cool!" Lily giggled, twirling a strand of her platinum hair around her finger.

I glanced through the corner of my eye at Kaden, who was staring at the two girls with his face scrunched up in annoyance. His nostrils flared, and his hands were clenched into tight fists on top of the table. I expected smoke to come out of his ears at any second. I tried to figure out why he was so angry, and I realized that it must have been the mention of Simon and our date. I quickly turned my attention back to Brittany and Lily, not wanting to watch Kaden boil over. He should know by now that I only went out with Simon to make him jealous.

Brittany blew a bubble with her gum before continuing, "Yeah. We totes thought that you were like a loser, but since you were able to land a date with Simon and now this hottie, it's obvious that you are like totes cool."

Utterly confused, I looked back and forth between the two. Slowly, I tilted my head to the side and tried, "Thank you?"

Lily waved a dismissive hand. "Listen. There's this party at Chad Bryant's house later tonight. Everyone's ditching school today to get ready for it, and I'm sure everyone will be too hungover to go to school tomorrow. Why don't you put on some cute clothes like you've been wearing to school and like totes come since you're cool now? It'll be loads of fun!"

It took me a few seconds to process their words. This was actually happening. I was being invited to the "cool kids" party. I had wanted to be included like this for so long, and one of my biggest dreams was to have friends who would invite me to things. I couldn't believe how much my world was changing. Everything that I knew to be real was changing, including my luck with friends.

Still in utter disbelief, I muttered, "Sure."

"Sweet! See you there!" Brittany said. They each gave me a friendly wave as they linked arms and walked out.

I turned back to Kaden with a smile glued to my lips, but as soon as my eyes found his, it quickly faded. He was glaring at me with narrowed slits for eyes, and his arms were crossed over his chest.

"What?" I asked.

"You are not going to that party."

I scoffed at him and took a sip of my coffee. "Why not?"

"Because all of those people are bad influences."

"Says the fallen angel," I glared.

As soon as the words left my mouth his face fell, and he drew back from me, uncrossing his arms. My stomach twisted in a tight knot as I realized the amount of venom that statement held for him. Wishing that I could take those words back, I covered my mouth with both hands. I hadn't meant that. I'd just been so hurt by the fact that he couldn't see this was a chance for me to make friends, which was something I had wanted for a long time. He had confided in me his biggest secret, something that had torn at him, and I'd just used it against him. What kind of horrible person was I?

My eyes grew moist with the threat of tears as I shook my head, pleading, "Kaden, I'm so sorry. I didn't mean that. I swear that I didn't! I just said that in the heat of the moment. I promise you!"

Clearly hurt, he looked away from me. His usually bright eyes had turned down, matching the frown he now wore. I tried reaching for his hand, but he pulled away from me. Standing up, he gathered his half-eaten bagel and coffee, threw it away, then walked out. I buried my face in my hands, wanting so badly to cry, but I refused to let anyone here see me. I was frustrated with myself, and the thought of losing Kaden because of this terrified me. Not knowing what else to do, I threw my coffee away before racing outside after him.

As soon as I stepped outside, my eyes darted all around me in search of his figure, but I didn't see him anywhere among the crowd. I swallowed hard as my mind raced to think of where he would've gone. The first place that came to mind was his warehouse, so I darted off in that direction.

When I had distanced myself from town and made it to the deserted street that led to Kaden's warehouse, I became lost in my thoughts. I couldn't believe that I'd said that to Kaden, especially after everything he had done for me. Being upset in the heat of the moment was no excuse. He didn't deserve such harsh words.

I mean, yes, I wanted Kaden to be happy for me. I was finally starting to make friends, people who actually wanted me around. Granted, it wasn't until I went out with Simon and started dressing nice that they'd wanted to be around me. When I really thought about it, Kaden was the only one who was there for me before the clothes and date. He was my friend, my *real* friend. He was someone who genuinely cared, and I had thrown it back in his face.

Determined to make things right between us, I straightened. As I passed by a large tree, a figure dropped down from the branches above. I jumped as he landed in a crouch in front of me. My heart stopped as the person stood up, and I came face to face with Landon. Standing tall in order to tower over me, he smiled down into my horrified eyes.

"Well, hello Raven. Good to see you again. Miss me?"

Panic washed over me, and I shrank away from him. My heart pounded in my chest as I quickly darted to the side in an attempt to run past him, but he dashed in front of me again, an amused grin lighting his face. "I'm only here to talk. I don't want to hurt you. But if you would like to try to run, then be my guest. I don't mind playing cat and mouse. Just so you know though, I'm the cat, and the cat always wins."

I swallowed hard, and he obviously heard it because his grin became more amused, more sinister. My body trembled as fear welled up inside of me, but I couldn't let him see that. It would only give him more power.

"So," I started, rage rushing out with each word, "this is all a game to you? Chasing me, kidnapping me, trying to kill me?"

He chuckled and said, "That's actually why I wanted to

talk to you. This whole subject about killing you has me thinking a lot."

I studied him, fearing he would try to kill me in some way within the next few moments. He only looked at me expectantly, obviously waiting for me to push him for answers. When I didn't, he cleared his throat and stood up straighter. "So, I'm assuming that after that little incident the other night, Kaden came clean to you about everything? Told you the truth?"

I crossed my arms, faking a confidence that I didn't actually feel. "You mean the truth about fallen angels? The truth about how you and your gang of flying freaks are evil and have been trying to kill me for no reason? Then yes, he did tell me."

Landon smiled and began walking in a small circle around me as if I was the prey that he was going to pounce on at any moment. I remained rooted to my spot out of fear that if I moved even slightly, he would attack.

He chuckled behind me and said, "Interesting. And did your hero tell you just which of my men it was who came after you all of those times? Or perhaps *why* he did it?" He circled back around to stand in front of me once more, and he reached out to touch a strand of my hair. I recoiled from his touch, and bile rose up in my throat with the urge to vomit.

He laughed at my reaction to him as a darkness passed over his features. "He clearly didn't, since you're still there with him."

My eyes bore into his as I tried to piece together what

he meant by that. Kaden had said he didn't know who it was that came after me or why they did it. There was no reason for that to make me not want to stay with him. The longer I was left to think about it though, the more Landon's words were beginning to formulate ideas in my head, and I was positive they were lies. It could never be true.

I glared at him and shoved him away from me. "Go to hell!" I spat out.

He glowered at me and whispered, "I'd watch your tongue, girl."

He swung a fist at me, punching me in the middle of my stomach. I doubled over in pain as my breath left me. Dropping to my knees, I clutched my stomach as Landon kneed me in the face, sending me to lie flat on my back. Letting out a moan of agony, I clutched my eye where his knee had collided. Warm blood seeped through my fingers where he had busted my brow open. I sucked in a gulp of air, trying to keep myself from crying. Pain welled up under my hand, but I didn't want to give him the satisfaction of seeing me cry.

He got down on one knee, and he picked me up by my hair to a sitting position. He drew his fist back, preparing to throw it at my face again, so I readied my fists in an attempt to swing at him first. But before either of us could make a move, a deep, low growl emitted from the trees nearest to us. We both whipped our heads around towards the sound, and my breathing stopped when I laid eyes on the source of the low, deep rumble.

My voice was barely audible as I mumbled, "It can't be."

Chapter Seventeen

MY HEART POUNDED AS a jet black wolf with crystal blue eyes emerged from the cover of the trees. It was the same wolf from that day two years ago! Instead of the caring, compassionate creature from that day though, he was baring his teeth and growling in a way that sent chills up my spine. His face was scrunched around his eyes as he stared at his prey, and his body was crouched low to the ground in a stance that displayed his readiness to attack.

Landon dropped my hair, letting me fall back to the asphalt. He took a slow step away from me, and his dark, menacing eyes never left the large beast. That movement was enough for the wolf though. His prey had moved, so he did too.

The wolf leapt towards us, and his extended claws missed Landon by only a few inches. The beast's eyes narrowed at Landon as his dark wings sprung from his back, ripping his shirt from his torso. He didn't seem to notice though. He took to the sky as the wolf leapt at him once more, catching Landon's foot in his mouth.

Landon cried out and kicked at the wolf's face in an attempt to make him let go. That just made the monstrous beast angrier, and he began shaking Landon like a rag doll. Blood was pouring down from his ankle as the giant beast pulled him closer to the ground. Landon struggled to fight off the wolf as he quickly pulled out a gun from his back pocket. A gasp escaped from my lips, and my heart seemed to stop beating as he aimed it at the wolf.

"No!" I screamed, jumping to my feet.

A desperate need to get the gun away from Landon swam through me as I ran towards them, but before I could make it to where they continued to fight, the deafening bang from the gun exploded around us. I stopped dead in my tracks as the wolf let out a whimper, and slowly, he let go of Landon's foot. His large body slumped to the ground with a heavy smack.

Landon turned quickly, flying away from us as I ran towards the wolf. Tears flooded my eyes, and my body shook with heavy sobs. I dropped to my knees beside him, slowly reaching my shaking hands out towards his furry body. His eyes were shut, and blood was seeping from his shoulder. He was breathing softly though, which meant he was still alive. For now.

As I placed my hands in the wolf's soft fur, his eyes slowly fluttered open to look into mine. The moment our eyes locked, realization hit me like a heavy blow. My heart fell as I figured out exactly what was going on. I leaned down into his fur as heavy sobs racked my body. I held on tightly to his soft coat as the fear of him dying plagued me. He couldn't die.

"I'm-" I choked through sobs. "I'm so sorry. You- you shouldn't have done that."

He started to lift up, so I scooted back slightly to look up at him. He wobbled as he stood up weakly, and he was careful to avoid standing on his front right paw, which connected to the shoulder where he was shot. His crystal blue eyes met mine once more before he leaned forward to nuzzle my cheek with his. I grasped onto the fur around his neck, burying my face in his good shoulder. He broke away from me as he quickly turned and ran back into the shadows of the trees.

Tears continued to stream down my face as I assembled what to do in my head. My own wounds were long forgotten at this point, and the only thing I could think about was the need to get to Kaden. I had to get to his warehouse. I leapt to my feet and pumped my legs harder than I ever had as I raced the rest of the way there. When I darted inside, the sound of water running echoed from the bathroom.

I sped to the bathroom door with a knot in my throat. My breathing was erratic from running all the way here, so I tried to calm it back down to normal. I needed to remain composed.

Taking a deep breath, I called, "Kaden?"

There was a pause. He cleared his throat and said in a gruff voice, "Yeah?"

I tried the knob, but it was locked. I beat my fist on the

door. "Let me in!"

He didn't respond. My throat tightened. The image of his unconscious or lifeless body flashed behind my eyes, so I took a couple of steps away from the door and ran at it. Throwing my body into the door as hard as I possibly could, it fell in. The sound of splintering wood filled the space as I landed in a heap on the floor by the sink. I shook my head, trying to clear the dizziness out of it that I had just created. Thank God that my adrenaline dulled the pain that I surely would've felt otherwise.

When I looked up, Kaden's wide eyes stared down at me as he leaned against the shower wall. He was using it as support in order to stand upright. I kept my eyes on his upper half because I could see that he was clearly naked, but I didn't even have time to think about that. Blood was pouring from his right shoulder where a small but gaping wound was.

I quickly rose to my feet and stumbled towards him as he tried to turn away from me, but that movement made him lose his support of the wall. He began to fall towards the bottom of the shower until I reached out and caught him. He sagged in my arms as I held him close, the hot water soaking us both.

My tears mixed with the water raining down as I brushed his hair back from his forehead. His breathing was shallow, and I slowly reached towards his wound, wishing that my touch could heal it away. I stopped short of brushing my fingers across it and looked back into his half-shut eyes.

With tears streaming down my face, I begged, "Why

did you do that, Kaden? Why didn't you just let him go?"

He gave a slow shake of his head and asked, "How- how did you know it was me?"

I gave a small, sad laugh as I cupped his cheek. "Your eyes. I always knew that they looked familiar. I've never seen blue eyes like yours."

My eyes remained locked with his as he slowly brought his hand up to wipe away a tear that was slipping down my cheek. "Please don't cry," he whispered.

This only made the tears flow more as I clenched my eyes shut and pushed my cheek harder into his hand. When I opened them again, my eyes grew wide. I froze as the hole in his shoulder slowly began to grow back together. The skin was reknitting itself, and the blood washed away with the steamy water. He moved his shoulders in small circles as it closed all the way. He looked at his shoulder then at me, a grin spreading across his lips.

"Ta-da!" he laughed.

He sat up as my mouth dropped open. He stood, turning off the water as he went. Grabbing a towel off of the sink, he wrapped it around his lower half before coming back to pick me up out of the shower. I was so dumbfounded by what had just happened that my body refused to move. He'd just healed right before my eyes! His skin had stitched itself together!

I stared at his shoulder in disbelief as he carried me to the sink. He sat me on the edge of the counter, looking intently at my split open brow, but I couldn't focus on that. I wasn't able to tear my eyes away from the place where his gunshot wound had been just moments ago.

He laughed and turned my face to look him in the eyes. These were eyes that I had seen before now, even before just a few months ago. Those endless gems of blue that tugged gently on my heart had always looked familiar, and now I knew why. They were the blue eyes that had filled me with love and protection two years ago.

"Would you stop staring like that?" he chuckled. "It's fine. Angels heal relatively fast. I was hoping it would heal before you got here, but you run very fast."

He leaned down to pull a first aid kit out from under the sink. In doing so, he was forced to crouch down, and his perfectly sculpted back was exposed to my view. That was when I saw it. Resting in between his shoulder blades was a beautifully drawn and detailed depiction of a wolf.

As he stood back up and placed the medical kit next to me, my eyes studied him. Small drops of water continued to slide down the length of his black hair before rolling down his face and onto his tanned body. I swallowed hard, trying to keep my feelings at bay for now.

His gentle eyes were focused on my brow as he carefully dabbed at it with a cotton ball. I stared into those amazing eyes of his as he concentrated. Swallowing, I whispered, "That was you that day. In the woods. You were the wolf that was there for me two years ago."

I already knew the answer, which is why I wasn't asking. I was confronting him. More than anything, I wanted to hear him admit that it was him. He was, he *is*, the wolf.

His hand paused as he slowly met my gaze. He stared

into my eyes for what felt like an eternity as he debated what to say. My determined gaze never faltered from his, so he relented by giving me a small nod.

I leaned closer and asked, "So did you recognize me when we met that day at the bookstore? Or at school, even?"

He smiled at me and said, "I did. That was one of the reasons I couldn't be an asshole to you forever." I smiled at that because he was acknowledging the fact that he'd been a jerk at first. Upon seeing me smile, his grin deepened. He tucked a strand of my hair behind my ear before continuing. "I remembered you very well. How could I not remember someone as beautiful as you?"

I ducked my head, and my stomach flipped. My entire body and cheeks began buzzing with a surreal warmth. He thought I was beautiful, and in that moment, I had never felt more beautiful. I looked back up at him to find him leaning in close, watching me with a smile.

"It's crazy to think that I met you so long ago." I smiled. "What were you doing here?"

"Believe it or not, one of my charges actually lives here. I was here watching her when I found you that day. I-" he paused, looking away. "I was still an angel then." His face fell again, and he closed his eyes at the memory.

I cupped his cheeks in my hands and raised his face, forcing him to look at me with those eyes again. I couldn't bear seeing his eyes dull with sadness. I always wanted them to shine. I leaned forward to softly brush my lips across his. It was enough to make him grin again. I smiled back at him as he worked to patch up my brow with gauze and medical tape.

My eyes never left his as I asked, "So you were here protecting your charge? Do I know them?"

He tilted his head a bit, as though he were contemplating something. "Yes, you know her."

Her. It was a girl. Could it be the one he'd fallen in love with? A twinge of jealousy shot through me as I asked, "Who is she? What's her name?"

He finished smoothing down the medical tape over my brow, and he stepped back to give his handiwork an approving nod. I watched as his eyes traveled down to mine, and he grew serious. "Did he hurt you anywhere else?"

He hadn't answered my question, but that was fine. I would find out eventually, and honestly, I wasn't too excited to hear the answer. I shook my head. "You shouldn't be worried about me though. You're the one who was shot."

I looked back at his shoulder again, letting my eyes trail over his bare chest and down his sculpted stomach. My cheeks grew red as my gaze met the hem of the towel that hung dangerously low on his hips. Clearing my throat, I looked back towards the shower.

Searching for something to say that would cover up my staring at his half-naked body, I asked, "Does water help heal you faster or something?"

He laughed. "No. Why?"

I shrugged as I found the courage to look at him once more. "You were in the shower, so I thought that maybe the water helped to heal you."

He gave a small, measured nod as understanding spread across his features. He smiled and said, "I got in the shower hoping to heal and wash the blood off before you made it here. I figured that if you got here before I was done healing, you would hear the shower and not come in." He gestured to the door hanging off its hinges before adding with a smirk, "Clearly, I was wrong."

I looked down sheepishly. "Sorry about your door. I was just worried that you were dying."

I looked at him again, and my mind replayed the moment when I'd realized Kaden was the wolf. I'd been so terrified of losing him in that instant. The only thing I could think about was the fact that Kaden had been shot. Adrenaline had shot through my body, and there was only that desperate need to get to him. I had to make sure he was okay, and I refused to let myself think the worst until I saw him with my own eyes. I cared for him so much, and the thought of him hurt pained me.

The idea of Kaden in pain reminded me of the way we left things at the cafe. I closed my eyes and looked down as the guilt washed over me again. "Kaden, I am so sorry for the thing I said this morning. I didn't mean it. You *have* to know that I didn't mean it."

A tear brimmed over my eyes, and it slowly streaked down my cheek. Kaden stepped closer to me, and he reached out to brush it away with the back of his warm hand. He crooked his finger under my chin, tilting it up to where our eyes could meet.

He gently kissed my forehead, his soft lips brushing across my skin as he whispered, "I know. You don't have to be sorry."

He pulled back to meet my eyes again, continuing, "That's why I left. I didn't want to say something that I didn't mean either and hate myself for it later." Anger crossed his face as his eyes flicked to the wound above my brow. "But that was dumb. I never should've left you. I was just coming back when I saw you and Landon. That's when he hit you."

Kaden's gaze traced down my body before stopping on my stomach, and I remembered the feeling of the wind being knocked out of me. One thing was for sure, Landon hadn't held anything back when he swung at me. Kaden's eyes traveled back up until they found mine. "When I saw him hit you like that, I lost it. I transformed into a wolf before I even knew what I was doing. After that, all I remember is charging after him in a blind rage."

He still looked livid as the memory replayed behind his eyes, so I climbed down from the sink to stand before him. I wrapped my arms around his wet torso and looked up at him. I didn't know what else to do to make the anger leave his features, so I said, "I'm okay."

I let his arms wrap around me and hold me tight against him. I was starting to become very aware of the fact that the only thing covering him was a towel, which could easily be removed.

"What did he say to you?" Kaden asked, cutting off my wandering thoughts.

I sighed and stepped back from him. Crossing my arms, I leaned against the sink. "That's actually something I needed to talk to you about."

He stepped closer to me, which caused the towel to slip

down a bit lower. I couldn't help myself from staring at the sculpted V that was starting to show. My cheeks flushed as I heard him laugh softly, no doubt catching me staring. He moved so that we were pressed together again, and he looked down at me with a gleam in his eye.

"What is it?" he asked.

I swallowed, getting my thoughts back on track. "Well, Landon told me to ask you again who it was that attacked me." Kaden's face remained blank when I said this, but I saw something change in his eyes. They suddenly turned darker, with an intense seriousness, which I could tell he was trying hard to hide. "He said you knew who it was."

Kaden tilted his head towards me, making me get distracted again. He started softly pecking at my neck, sending a tingling sensation throughout my body. I closed my eyes, relishing in the soft kisses he was trailing up my skin. I couldn't get distracted though.

I opened my eyes, trying to concentrate, "The- uh- the way he talked about it," I paused again as his hands slipped onto my waist, tugging me further into him. I swallowed hard, trying to finish. "He made it sound like you-"

There was no chance for me to finish. Kaden pulled away from my neck to bring his lips down on mine. Immediately, all my thoughts melted away. There was only me and him.

I wrapped my fingers into his hair as our kiss deepened in a gentle way, which kept my cut lip from hurting. He grabbed my hips, and in one swift motion, he picked me up and wrapped my legs around his waist. He turned, carrying me to the bed. His lips traced down my neck again as we collapsed onto the mattress. I let my hands slide down his back, meeting the hem of the towel. That piece of cloth was quickly getting on my nerves.

Kaden brought his lips down on mine again, sliding his tongue into my mouth. My hands trailed down his chest and stomach as he slid his hand underneath my shirt. As his hand went up further, mine went down lower until it touched the wet fabric of the towel. I gently tugged at it until Kaden slowly pulled back to look at me.

I looked into his light blue eyes as he stared into my green ones. His chest rose and fell against mine, wetting my shirt. I didn't care though. I wanted the shirt to be gone anyways. I wanted us to be together, fully, which couldn't be done with clothes in the way. As he stared at me, I knew I saw longing in his eyes. He wanted me the way I wanted him, so I didn't understand why he stopped.

"Let's do something fun," he suddenly said.

I stared at him, trying to calm down my racing heart. *I thought we were.* "Like what?"

He smiled and said, "You'll see."

He stood, so I sat up. He grabbed a pair of what looked to be swimming trunks out of a makeshift closet. Walking into the bathroom, he emerged a few minutes later wearing the light blue trunks. His body looked amazing, and the blue of the swimming trunks made his eyes stand out even more. He looked flawless.

My eyes traced over him as he smiled, and I asked, "We're going swimming? It's cold outside."

He reached his hand out for me, and I reluctantly took it. He grabbed me around the waist and twirled me around to where my back was pinned against his chest. His breath brushed across my neck as he whispered, "I want to try something."

His wings shot out of his back, making my breath catch in my throat. The black, silky feathers rustled with the promise of flight, and I swallowed hard as excitement bubbled up in the pit of my stomach. I held my breath as the wings reached high above us, and with one large beat of the air, we rose off the ground and out the rooftop door.

Chapter Eighteen

KADEN KEPT LOW TO the trees and away from town as we flew in the direction of my trailer. I had no idea what he was planning, but at the moment, I was content. I loved flying. The wind blew all around me, but the adrenaline flowing through me kept the cold from registering in my mind. The trees were flying by us at an incredible speed as he moved even faster. I smiled to myself, thrilled to be in his arms, soaring through the air once more.

When we neared my house, he slowed. He circled my trailer before landing in front of my bedroom window. I looked at him expectantly, and he said with a laugh, "Go change into a bathing suit."

Raising a brow, I noted, "Like I said before, it's cold outside. What do I need a swim suit for?"

"Nope. No questions. Just trust me."

I rolled my eyes, which just made him grin more. He helped me climb through the window, and when I got inside, I shut my curtains so he couldn't watch me change. I went over to my dresser and opened the drawers in search of a bathing suit. I never went swimming, so I didn't have very many suits. They were all from a couple years ago, so I just hoped that at least one would fit.

I found a bikini that I'd bought when I was fifteen, but it was black with flowers all over it. I quickly tossed it aside. The next one I found was from when I was thirteen. It was a one piece that sported a pink fabric with frogs scattered across every inch of it. I threw that one aside too.

I finally came to the one I was searching for. I had gotten it two years ago, when I was sixteen. It was a silver bikini, which reminded me of the moonlight from the night Kaden and I had flown for the first time. I just prayed that it would still fit.

I carefully worked to shrug my clothes off the way Kaden had earlier, and was relieved when I managed to do it with no hint of pain. I stepped into the bikini, silently praying that one of Kaden's abilities was not x-ray vision. It wouldn't have surprised me if it was though.

Once I was finished putting it on, I stepped in front of the mirror. The swim suit did very little to cover my breasts, which had grown a bit since I'd been sixteen, but that just made it look even sexier. My black curls were cascading down my back, making my skin look even more alabaster than normal.

I would've looked beautiful if it wasn't for all the bruises and cuts on my legs, arms, and stomach. The place where Chesed had brought his knife down on me was still a healing mess of stitches. It remained red around the wound, but it didn't look as bad as what I would've thought. I could probably thank Kaden's stitching skills for that.

Unfortunately, there were other injuries too. A purple bruise was forming where Landon had punched me in the abdomen, and my brow was covered with the bandage that Kaden had used to patch up the place where it was busted. The same eye had a purple tint around it from Landon's blow. On top of all that, small cuts and bruises dotted along other places on my body where the group of fallen angels had beaten me that night.

I closed my eyes at my reflection as I dreaded the moment when Kaden would see the disaster that painted my skin. I went to my closet and grabbed an extra large t-shirt that covered my body. My legs were still exposed, but they didn't look as bad as my upper half.

I sighed heavily as I opened the curtains to climb out of the window. Kaden helped me down with a smile plastered on his lips. It contained an intense amount of joy behind it, and seeing him so genuinely happy made my heart flutter. I smiled back at him as he took my hand and led me towards the woods.

"Why are we going into the woods?" I asked.

He looked back at me with a smirk and said, "You're about to find out."

As we continued to trek further into the trees, I realized we were walking in the direction of my clearing. The further we walked, the closer we got. That's when it hit me. He wanted to swim in the pond. My eyes found his as we walked side by side, and he looked at me with a twinkle in his gaze.

I smiled up at him, unable to contain my grin when he looked at me that way.

When we stepped through the trees and into my safe haven, Kaden looked around it just as he had last time. I matched his expression as I took in the beautiful scenery. It felt good to be back, and it felt even better to be here with him next to me. I glanced at him as he swallowed hard, but he quickly recovered from whatever he was feeling with a smile. He never released my hand as he approached the waiting pond. He dipped his foot in then quickly pulled it back out.

A shiver ran through him as he looked at me, laughing. "You were right, it's definitely cold. But I think I have a way to fix that."

I watched him in fascination as he squatted next to the clear water. Concentrating, he put his hand in and closed his eyes. He held his hand in a fist under the water, and after a few moments, he opened his hand up to wave it under the water's surface. As his open palm moved under the frigid water, it began to bubble, and steam began to rise from the ripples. He stood, smiling down at me.

I stared at him in amazement. "You heated the water!"

The sound of his gentle laugh surrounded me as he nodded. Stepping closer to me, he pressed our bodies together and grabbed at the bottom of my shirt. He slowly slipped it over my head, revealing my bikini. Letting the shirt fall from his hands, his hungry eyes took in every inch of me.

My nerves were rising the more his eyes traced me, and the way he took my shirt off felt incredibly intimate. His hand slowly moved along the bruises on my arms, chest, and stomach. Anguish quickly replaced his elation as he looked into my eyes.

"I'm so sorry this happened to you."

I lifted my arms to wrap them around his neck. "It's not your fault, Kaden."

He closed his eyes and rested his forehead against mine. "It is though. If I had left sooner then they wouldn't have known that you-" He stopped talking, his body growing rigid.

I raised a skeptical eyebrow. "Wouldn't have known I what?"

He drew back from me, smiling at me again. He shook his head. "Nothing. Come on. Let's get in."

Grabbing my hand, he backed into the water, letting it slip around his feet, then knees, then waist. He tugged me along with him until we both stood on the soft, smooth pebbles that filled the bottom of the pond. The warm water kissed me all over, and I closed my eyes, relishing in its incredible heat. When I opened my eyes again, I found Kaden watching me with a soft smile.

"What?" I asked, blushing.

"You are so beautiful."

I bit my lip and looked away as heat colored my cheeks. I waded further into the water until it came up to my chest. He followed me, his gaze watching me closely. I swallowed hard as his eyes were beginning to get a hungry passion in them. I could feel the intensity of it growing, which in turn sent my nerves into a frenzy.

"So," I said, trying to calm the butterflies in my stomach. I needed to talk about something in order to keep myself calm, so I said the first thing that came to my mind. "Was your charge who lived here the girl that you fell in love with?"

He furrowed his brow at my question, closing all the distance between us. I held my breath and stared into his eyes as I waited for his answer. Instead of answering me directly though, he nodded. I swallowed hard and took a step back from him as I skimmed my hand on top of the water in an attempt to remain calm. I turned my back to him. I knew I shouldn't feel jealous, but I did.

Looking back over my shoulder at him, I asked, "What was she like?"

He watched me as he took another measured step towards me, and this closed the distance between us, allowing him to put his chest to my back. He circled his arms around me under the water and held me close.

"Well, for one, she was beautiful. Very beautiful." My heart clenched. "Besides that, she was very strong. She had a lot of courage and strength inside of her." Of course she was strong, unlike me. I was nothing but a terrified fool who was always crying and too afraid to ever do anything. "She was also incredibly kind-hearted, always caring for others. Putting their needs and feelings above her own."

I looked down into the water at his hands clasped around my stomach, which began to move lower to touch the top of my bikini bottoms. I swallowed and mumbled, "You talk about her as if she was perfect."

He didn't say anything, but he kissed my bare shoulder as his finger hooked onto the bottoms I was wearing. My knees grew weak as he slowly started to tug them lower. I closed my eyes, not wanting to know the answer to my next question, but knowing that I needed to before things escalated.

I turned to face him, and he smiled at me in his charming way. My heart melted as he lowered his mouth towards mine. When his lips were close enough for our breath to intertwine, I whispered, "Do you still love her?"

Without hesitating, he said the one word that I was praying he wouldn't. "Yes."

My face scrunched up in a mix of anger and pain. I quickly shoved him away from me, and he frowned at me with a confused raised brow. "What's wrong?" he asked.

I turned to get out of the water, and I angrily grabbed my t-shirt to throw it on. I looked back at him with tears brimming my eyes. "How can you do that? How can you try to act like you have feelings for me and try to get in my pants when you love someone else? I kept telling myself that you cared about me. I kept trying to convince myself that there was something there other than you wanting to get some, but I was clearly wrong. Go back to the one you love Kaden! I won't let you toy with my feelings anymore!"

I turned and stormed back towards my house. Tears streamed down my cheeks the entire way, and the ache in my heart tightened in my chest. I knew Kaden could catch me if he wanted to, but he was nowhere in sight. He wasn't coming to catch up with me to explain away everything. He wasn't coming to comfort me or to mend my heart that he'd broken. It wasn't me he loved. It never was. This thought made my heart ache more, and my crying became even more violent.

Kaden was worse than Simon.

As soon as I made it to the trailer, I ran in through the front door. My dad was standing by his recliner, but when he saw me come in, his expression turned icy as he glared at me.

"Mandy?" he asked, growing visibly angrier by the second. His fat face was turning red, and his fists were clenched in tight balls. His body actually started shaking as he took an angry step towards me.

I tried calming my crying as I said, "No, dad. It's me, Raven. Your daughter."

He shook his head. "I can't stand this anymore! Get out! Get out of my head, and get out of my house, Mandy! Stay away from me!"

He raised his hand, bringing it down hard on my cheek. I let out a muffled grunt as I tumbled to the ground, and I clutched my now throbbing jaw. I was unable to stop the violent tears that cascaded down my face, which only seemed to fuel his fit more. He grabbed a fistful of my hair and yanked on it hard. I grabbed at his hands in a desperate attempt to make him let go. He dragged me to the door before throwing it wide open.

"Daddy, stop!" I cried.

He picked me up by my forearms, and he squeezed tight as he brought me up to his eye level. "Stay out of my life you dumb, fucking bitch!"

He pushed me as hard as he could, sending me falling backwards onto the gravel. I sobbed as I crawled back to the door, but before I made it, he slammed it shut on me. The click of the lock sliding into place caused my stomach to drop, and I raised up on my knees to bang on the door. I beat my fists against it, screaming and wailing for what felt like hours. After many long, silent moments, I rested my head against the door in defeat.

"Why is everything falling apart?" I whispered to myself as my tears continued to fall.

After remaining motionless for a few more moments, I slowly stood up, preparing to sneak into my room through the window. I could just lock myself in there until this drunken spell of his ended. Granted, he had never been this convinced that I was Mandy. He had also never thrown me out before, but I had nowhere else to go. Limping from landing on my ankle wrong, I walked around the house. I rounded the corner but stopped dead in my tracks when I saw who was waiting for me by the window.

"Well, don't you look pitiful," Landon said with a cocky smile.

Chapter Nineteen

I STARED AT LANDON, AND to my surprise, I didn't feel afraid. I felt so broken inside and out, so there wasn't much room left for anything else. If he wanted to end me then let him try. Life was hell for me at the moment, but I'd still go down fighting. It's crazy how I was still willing to fight despite my heart begging me to just give in to the eternal darkness.

I watched him, letting the tears roll down my cheeks. "If you're going to kill me then just get on with it. I want to get this fight over with."

He looked up towards the sky as though he were pondering it. Smiling wide, he finally looked at me again. "I'd love to. Really, I would, but I enjoy watching you suffer far too much. I mean after all, you did cause the strongest member of my group to leave, you almost got my men burned to death, and you made an animal nearly rip my foot off. I don't think you've suffered enough." He looked at me from head to toe then gave what he said a second thought.

"Or maybe you have? Did Kaden finally break your heart by telling you the truth about what he did?"

I stared at him, my brow furrowed in confusion. He'd broken my heart all right, but he'd never mentioned anything about him doing something. I looked down at my feet and answered, "No. Why don't you enlighten me? What did he do?"

Looking back at Landon, he smiled at me and said, "Go ask him for yourself. Once he's told you, you may come to me. I will gladly end you then, because believe me, you will want to die after what he's going to tell you. You know where to find me. I'm in the abandoned church."

His wings sprang out from his back with a loud smack. He lifted off the ground and flew at full speed towards me. I went to throw my hands up to brace myself for the impact, but his speed when flying was too fast for my eyes to even keep up with. His fist collided hard with my cheek, sending me to my knees on the ground outside my room. The world tilted beneath me, and dark spots clouded my vision. I swayed in the cold air before finally fading into the darkness.

***

When I finally forced my eyes open, it took me a moment to realize that it was dark outside. I was still lying face down outside my window, and the chill of the night air had numbed my body. I blinked my eyes a couple of times, and as I started shifting, I was able to register pain on every inch of me, both inside and out. The ache reached all the way to the deepest parts of me, and more than anything, I wanted to remain still in that one spot. I couldn't stay on the ground though. It was time for me to learn everything. I couldn't do this anymore. I had to go see Kaden. I had to make sure that my suspicions weren't true.

I slowly pushed myself up, only to have my arms fail me. I fell back to the ground with a heavy thud, and a mix of dirt and blood filled my mouth. Warm tears slipped down my cheeks as I laid there, and the urge to stay still called my name. The pain was overwhelming when I shifted, but I still needed to get to Kaden's.

I inhaled a large gulp of air as I tried to raise up again. At the same time, I heard the sound of wings flying above me, followed by the sound of feet touching the ground.

"Raven!" Kaden shouted as his gentle hands wrapped around my upper arms.

He kneeled down, helping me to come to a sitting position. As soon as I was upright, he scooped me up in his arms, holding me against his warm, bare chest. My cheek lulled against his shoulder as he whispered, "What happened?"

I couldn't respond though. The only answer he got out of me was a tear rolling down my cheek. His arms clung to me tighter. "Just hold on, Raven. I've got you," he whispered.

He took to the air, letting the cool wind wrap around me. I didn't want to feel him hold me this way. I didn't want him to act like he cared about me. I knew the truth about his feelings, and I was determined to find out the rest of the truth as soon as our feet were firmly on the ground.

I let myself rest in his arms as we flew through the night sky towards his place. I needed to build up some sort of strength for when I confronted him, because this wasn't going to be easy by any means. I was terrified because if things played out the way that Landon was implying, then the heartbreak I'd felt earlier would be nothing compared to the heartbreak I would feel.

When we finally landed, Kaden retracted his wings into his back. He looked down at me with worry written all over his face, but I didn't want to see that look because it was a lie. He wasn't really worried about me. He continued to watch me like that as we walked through the door.

As soon as we made it inside, my eyes fell upon the blanket that had been spread out in the center of the room. Candles were lit all around it with roses here and there. A plate of chocolate covered strawberries, my favorite food ever, was centered on the blanket, accompanied by a bottle of champagne with two glasses. The rafters had soft, fairy lights strung around them, aiding the candles in being the only source of light in the room. It was magical, beautiful, and romantic. I couldn't help but let my jaw drop slightly.

Kaden smiled softly at me. "Do you like it? This is what I was doing after you ran off today. I realized there was a misunderstanding, so I wanted to surprise you with something as I tried to explain myself. There are some things I need to tell you."

I didn't answer him, and I ignored his explanation. I couldn't let him distract me. Not this time.

I slowly moved to get out of his arms, and he carefully

let me back on my feet. My legs wobbled at first, so he held onto me with a furrowed brow. When I was sure I could stand without him, I looked into his eyes and backed several steps away from him.

He looked at me with sadness clouding his eyes. "Look, I know you're hurt by what happened today, but please, let me explain. It isn't what you think."

I closed my eyes, pushing aside that conversation. There was one I needed an answer to much more right now. "Was it you?"

"Was what me?" he asked, his features puzzled.

I looked back at him with angry tears brimming in my eyes. He watched me with an expectant gaze. A tear slipped past as I uttered the question that had been haunting me since Landon had planted it in my head. "Were you the one who tried to kill me?"

Kaden grew pale and rigid as he stared at me. My body shook as my fear and rage mounted. "Answer me, Kaden! Was it you? The night in the alley? At the Martinezes'? Was it all you?"

His gaze slowly fell to stare down at his shoes, and I could hear him swallow despite being feet apart. I held my breath, waiting for his answer, but the longer I waited, the more afraid I became that it was true.

I balled my hands into fists and screamed at him, "Kaden, you answer me right now! Was it you who tried to kill me?"

He scrunched his face up in remorse as he yelled, "Okay!" He let out a pained sigh as his distraught eyes found mine. "I-" he paused, looking at me with a deep frown. He swallowed hard and finished, "It was me. I-I was the one who tried to kill you."

My hands flew up to cover my mouth as a strangled gasp tried to escape me, and my anxiety skyrocketed. Kaden made a step towards me, but I quickly turned away to run from him. He was blocking the front door, and the bathroom door was broken, so the only place to go was up the stairs.

I darted for the steps in a desperate attempt to get away from him, but he quickly caught up to me. He grabbed me by the waist and pulled me against his chest. He wrapped his arms around me, pinning my arms to my sides.

That night in the alley flashed back into my mind - this was the way I struggled then too. I cried harder and screamed, beating my fists against his legs as he backed me away from the stairs. When we neared the bed, he pushed me down onto it. I was lying on my stomach, but he rolled me over and got on top of me to pin me down.

I struggled beneath him, crying and screaming as he said in a gentle voice, "Raven, please stop. Listen to me."

I panted as I turned my face away from him, refusing to meet his eyes. I was sobbing now, and I felt like my heart had been ripped from my chest. This couldn't be real. His grip loosened on my wrists, but it wasn't enough to allow me to break free. I continued panting and crying, wishing that this was all a nightmare, but I knew it wasn't. The pain was far too real.

"Please, Raven. Let me explain. There is more to it than what Landon has made you believe. You know that I would never hurt you."

I closed my eyes, my lip trembling. I hated his words because as much as I didn't want to believe them right now, I did. I had always believed that about him, even when he seemed like a jerk or even in moments like this. I had never, not once, believed that Kaden would *actually* hurt me. But I had to have been wrong because he had been the one who'd tried to kill me twice.

"Please, Raven," he whispered again.

After taking a few calming breaths, I slowly turned my eyes towards him. He was staring at me with grief, guilt, and hurt flooding his features. He gazed down at me and asked, "Will you please listen to what I have to say?"

I closed my eyes, knowing that I was about to give in to him. I couldn't help it. I loved him and wanted an explanation. Opening my eyes again, I slowly nodded.

He let go of the breath he was holding and carefully got off of me. He stood at the foot of the bed as I crawled to the head of it. I leaned against the wall, clutching a pillow in front of me as though that would shield me from anymore pain.

As I watched him run a shaky hand through his hair, I whispered, "Why, Kaden? Why did you try to kill me? I just don't understand."

He let his hands fall to his sides as his shoulders slumped forward in defeat. He looked back up at me slowly, his perfect, blue eyes staring into mine. Longing pushed its way forward, masking all the other emotions that he was showing. His eyes never left mine as he gave me a small, sad smile. "Because Raven. You are the reason I fell."

Chapter Twenty

MY EYES BORE INTO Kaden as I fought to understand. Surely I had misheard him. "What? No. You said you fell because-" I stopped, staring into his eyes. He still had that small smile on his lips, but it didn't quite meet his eyes. They were dulled with some sort of sadness. Could it be true?

He moved to sit down on the foot of the bed across from me. He kept his eyes carefully locked on mine as he said, "It was you, Raven. You were my charge. I was your guardian angel, and I've watched over you ever since you were born. That's why I was so confused when you pushed me away at the pond today. I thought you knew I was talking about you."

I slowly shook my head. I didn't think he was talking about me. After all, his description of this girl did not fit me in the slightest. "But the things you said when I told you to describe her didn't sound anything like me."

He laughed in that charming, gentle tone and said,

"You told me to describe the girl I fell in love with. I told you how I see you, not how you see yourself. You may not see someone beautiful, brave, and kind, but when I look at you, that's all I see."

I couldn't tear my eyes away from his as I worked to process his words. I couldn't believe this. Kaden was in love with me? For how long had he loved me? As his crystal eyes watched me with a buried sparkle, I could feel the love growing behind his gaze. No wonder I'd felt something between us from the moment I met him. He was my freaking guardian angel! That explained a lot, but it still didn't explain why he tried to kill me.

As if reading my thoughts, he let out a sigh and said, "Let me explain everything to you. From the beginning."

He slowly inched towards me, and his eyes met mine in a silent question, asking if it was all right for him to come closer. When I didn't object, he crawled the rest of the way over before sitting directly in front of me. Our knees touched, and he gave another long breath.

Looking back into my eyes, he began, "So, as a guardian angel, I had three charges. You were one of them. I had a duty to protect each of you, but even from the beginning, I had a soft spot for you. Watching you run around as a little girl, it just always seemed to make me smile, especially when you would go into the woods and we would play together. I thought of you as my first friend, something angels don't really have."

My eyes grew wide, and my mind flashed back to when I was little. Anytime I went into my clearing, I would always talk and laugh with my imaginary friend, and it always made me feel better no matter what was going on. Now I could see he wasn't imaginary at all.

"You were the one I would always talk to? I thought I always heard a voice, but I just brushed it aside as the wind in the trees."

He smiled and shook his head. "It wasn't the wind. It was me. I would speak back to you, and I loved seeing the way it made you happy."

He frowned as his shoulders sagged with the weight of something painful. He slowly shook his head as he added, "It seemed like the only time you were ever happy was when you were in that clearing talking to me."

I looked away from him because his words reminded me of all the heartache I used to feel anytime I was away from that clearing. He was right. The only time I ever felt happy or safe was when I was in that wide open space, running around, talking, and laughing with the voice in the wind. Things at home were bad now, but when I was younger, it felt so much worse. I wasn't able to face it then the way I did now, so my escape was always my imaginary friend. Everything changed though when Kaden came that day in the form of the wolf. After that, it never felt the same.

"As you got older," he continued, "and started growing up, I found myself always trying to find ways to come back to be with you. Granted, your case needed more attention than the others, but soon I was just coming for selfish reasons. I began neglecting my other charges because I wanted to constantly be there to protect you and keep you safe from anything that tried to hurt you.

"When you got to be around sixteen, things really changed. Suddenly, I started seeing you as more than just a dear friend. I saw how beautiful, caring, and amazing you were, so I couldn't resist my feelings for you at that point. I came to you that day in the form of the wolf because I wanted to comfort you as more than just an unseen figure in the trees. I needed to be more than just a voice who talked through the wind. I wanted to actually be *there*, but I knew I couldn't expose my angelic form. The only other option was to go to you as a wolf."

He swallowed hard. "That was when Heaven had enough. They knew that I had fallen in love with you, a human, so as punishment, they cast me out. That's also why when you came back, it didn't feel the same anymore. It was because the aura I'd placed around the clearing disappeared as I began my fall."

"Is that why you seemed so sad when we went to the clearing the first time?" I asked as the memory played in my mind. My mind replayed the way he'd looked around at it, and at the time, I'd felt like his reaction didn't make any sense. Now it was making perfect sense.

He nodded and looked down at his hands with pain written across his face. He was most likely thinking back to the moment when he was thrown out, forcing him to leave me and the clearing. Quietly, I asked, "Did it hurt? You know, when you were falling?"

He gave a bitter laugh and said, "Like Hell." His eyes found mine again. "But after the first couple months of descending, I finally passed out, so I didn't have to feel it the whole way down."

My eyes grew wide, and a sharp pain grasped at my heart. "Months?"

He had fallen and been in pain for *months*? How long did it even take to fall? Obviously it took awhile since he'd shown up two years after having started to fall. And it was all because of me.

He brushed my question aside and gave me a warm smile. "It's funny. The whole time I was blacked out, all I could do was dream of you. I pictured being able to meet you as myself for the first time. What it would be like to hold you, kiss you, have a life with you. That's all I wanted."

He looked away from me again as something dark fell over his face. "But as soon as I landed, that changed. When I opened my eyes and began my introduction with Landon, all I felt inside was rage and hate."

"At- at me?" I stuttered.

He nodded. "Falling changes angels. All the goodness and purity that you have as an angel gets stripped away and replaced with the exact opposite. It usually consumes them with anger and hate. It's like," he paused, trying to come up with the best way to describe what it was like. "It's like you're in this fog. You can't actually see clearly. All you see is a blur of red, searing anger that encompasses everything. I didn't even recognize you at first because everything was just stained *red*."

He gave a bitter laugh, shaking his head. "Can you believe that? I watched over you for sixteen years, and I couldn't even recognize you past all the hate and anger I felt. Anyways, in my case, a lot of my anger stemmed from the fact that I loved you, yet you didn't even know I existed. I was essentially not real to you. I was furious at the situation, that I wasn't a human who could actually be with you, and Landon took advantage of that. He told me that I could join them in their quest for revenge if I could just kill one of God's children. They knew why I fell, so they chose you because they figured if I could kill the girl I loved beyond words then I could kill anyone. I could be their ultimate monster."

He paused before adding in a quiet voice, "They showed me how they wanted me to kill you by using Brendon as an example."

My stomach lurched with this news, and a tight grip formed around my throat. Poor Brendon had been killed, and in a way, it was my fault. Kaden's eyes found mine again, reading my horrified expression. Gently, he said, "Chesed was the one who killed him."

A tear fell onto my cheek, and guilt consumed me. Brendon died because of me. He was used as a pawn in getting to me. I had unknowingly led to an innocent boy's death. I hadn't known Brendon that well, but I knew he did not deserve the fate he'd met. No one did.

Kaden watched me cautiously as he reached his hand out to smooth the tear back from my cheek. I let him because in this moment, I needed his warmth. I needed the comfort that his presence always gave me.

Kaden leaned forward a bit as he continued, "So after I

was shown how I was supposed to end you, we just had to wait for our chance to strike, which was that night at the bookstore. I waited in the alley for you, and as soon as you passed, I went for it. I grabbed you, and I was trying to get my knife out of my pocket, but you were struggling so much that I needed both hands to hold you."

His eyes and mouth were turned down with a mask of grief. His features displayed an expression that resembled that of someone about to vomit. Letting out a shaky breath, he said, "To tell you the truth, I was still so angry that night that I was really going to go through with it. I was actually going to kill you, again, not knowing it was *you*. I was still in the fog at the time, so it was like you were just a random stranger to me. The only reason I stopped was because the people showed up. There was nowhere for me to run though, so I had to fly away."

My mind went back to the moment when people showed up that night. No one could figure out where my attacker went. It was as if he'd disappeared into thin air. Officer Greene even made a joke that the only way for my attacker to get away was for him to sprout wings and fly. If only Officer Greene knew.

"I'm so thankful people showed up when they did," Kaden said, still looking like he might get sick. He ran a shaky hand through his hair, letting me see just how much this pained him. That in itself showed me how sorry he was. "I don't know what I would have done if I'd gone through with it."

Silence fell over us as we both searched for something

to say. Finally, he cleared his throat before glancing at me once more. "After that night when I failed to kill you, Landon decided I needed to enroll in your school. He wanted me to develop a friendship with you so I could get close to you and strike. He thought that would hurt you even more. Giving you a friend to just have them turn on you and kill you.

"SoI did. But as I watched you during class, pieces of my memories of you started coming back. I recognized you, and I started to understand that something wasn't right with what I was doing. My mind was still slightly clouded, but it was clearing.

"Anyways, that night when I walked you to the Martinezes', I knew from watching you all those years that they didn't lock the basement door. I came in that way and cut the breaker off. When you came downstairs, well, you know what happened."

He stared off with the distant memory of that night. I remembered it too, much to my dismay. I absently rubbed at my neck, recalling the terrifying feeling of being choked. It had been one of the scariest feelings in the world - desperately wanting and craving to breathe, but not being able to take in a breath.

He looked down at his hands as he continued, "Landon's bright idea of making me interact with you at school backfired on him though, because when I was there trying to strangle you that night, I couldn't do it. All my feelings from before I had fallen resurfaced at school and on our walk to the Martinezes'. I couldn't do it. I couldn't kill you, so I got up and left before I hurt you any further.

"After I came back, Landon and the guys quickly found out that I didn't go through with it. They were piecing together the truth about my returning feelings, which I knew couldn't be good. Landon has never had an angel not go through with his dirty work, so they decided to accompany me the next time to ensure that I ended you."

My eyes found his as I narrowed them in confusion. "The next time? I wasn't attacked any other time besides when Landon and his freaks got a hold of me."

He looked at me with sadness brimming in his eyes. He sighed and said, "This attack wasn't the same as the others. Instead of coming at you as me, they had me do something a little different.

"I came into school the next day and pretended to not know what had happened to your neck. My anger was real though. I was angry at myself and at the other fallen angels. I didn't want to hurt you anymore, so I did what they asked, just with my own twist. Just as Landon instructed, I spent a few months with you, working to grow our bond. When they were satisfied with our progress, I asked you out to dinner."

The date was Landon's idea? My mind raced to put the puzzle pieces together. That night at the restaurant, I wasn't attacked directly. Even so, *someone* had locked me in that bathroom as the fire started. My eyes slowly met his again as I figured out what he was about to tell me.

"The plan was to find a way to keep you in the restaurant while I set it on fire. I knew all the guys were there watching, and if I didn't kill you, they would. So when you went to the bathroom, that fallen angel with blue hair, Malachi, locked it from the outside. He gave me the signal, so I started a fire in the kitchen and made it spread to the main restaurant. I directed it as far away from the bathroom as I could get it to allow enough time for the guys to leave.

"Once we made it outside and it had been a couple of minutes, they were sure there was no way you'd survived. The restaurant was ablaze by then, and I was starting to get afraid that my fire had been too much. They made the mistake of leaving before they were sure you were dead, but that was what I was hoping for.

"As soon as they were gone, I ran back inside to get you. When you were safe and I knew you were going to be okay, I told myself that I wasn't going to see you anymore. Landon and the guys thought that you were dead, and I had to keep it that way to protect you."

I swallowed, remembering that the next day he didn't come to school. He was keeping his distance, but I guess he decided he needed to officially break ties with me because the day after that was the day he told me he never wanted to see me again. He pushed me away to keep me safe from Landon and the other fallen angels.

I looked at him and asked, "Why didn't you stay away then? You still came to school the next day."

He scoffed and said, "Because when I saw what you were wearing and found out that you were going out with Simon, I couldn't contain how pissed I was. I came to see if it was true, and when I saw you with him and all those other guys, I nearly set the whole school on fire.

"I left, and even though I knew I needed to stay away to keep you safe, I couldn't do it. I decided I was going to follow you on your date, but I realized too late that I wasn't the only one following you. I don't know how they did it, but somehow they figured out you were still alive."

I nodded and said, "It was Chesed. I guess they felt like double checking to be sure I was gone because Chesed came to the bookstore the day before my date with Simon. When he saw me and found out who I was, he left without saying anything else."

He closed his eyes and mumbled, "I never should have left you alone." He shook the thought away as he looked back at me. "Anyways, when I realized where Simon was trying to take you after the movies that night, I flew ahead to the farmhouse to wait on you. I was going to define the meaning of the word pain to him, but when you didn't come, I got worried.

"I flew to your house, his house, and the bookstore. When I didn't find you anywhere, I knew they must have found you. I went to the church and looked in through the window as they were all over you, hurting you in any way they could." Grief flooded his face again, and I knew he blamed himself for what happened.

"When you found out what I really was, I still tried hiding the part about you being the one I fell in love with because I was afraid that it would lead to you figuring everything out, including the times I played a role in your almost dying."

He looked away from me again as he mumbled, "That's

218

also why I always stopped when things were becoming too intense between us. I was still lying to you, and I couldn't take anything from you, knowing that you still didn't know the full truth about everything."

I swallowed hard, taking in all of the new information. When I'd come here tonight, I'd expected to find out that Kaden was only here to murder me, but there really was much more to it than what Landon had implied. I couldn't exactly fault Kaden for what had happened. He wasn't in his right mind when he did those things; he was essentially under a spell, and only after meeting me again did the spell unbreak. After the change in him at the Martinezes', he'd put everything he had into protecting me and caring for me, just like he had when he was still my guardian angel.

I looked into his amazing blue eyes, feeling myself get lost in them. He fell for me. Actually *fell*. He had given up everything for me. He knew me more than anyone else on this earth, and he loved me above all others here.

The connection I felt towards him was growing stronger with each passing moment, and that pull made even more sense now that I knew the full truth. Everything was out in the open now, and I knew that despite the mistakes Kaden had made, they didn't compare to what I felt in my heart for him.

He was my angel, and I loved him, just as he loved me.

I slowly sat the pillow I had been holding down next to me. He watched me, his chest rising and falling with steady breaths as I closed all the space between us and sat on his lap. I wrapped my arms around his neck, and he slid his around my back as he hugged me to him. I buried my face in the crook of his shoulder, and he hugged me tightly, as though this would be the last time he would ever get to hold me.

"I'm so sorry," he breathed against my hair. I could hear his voice catch with the threat of tears.

When I looked at him, he straightened, refusing to let his eyes moisten. I cupped his cheek and whispered, "I forgive you. I will always forgive you because I love you."

As soon as the words left my mouth, a heat swelled in his eyes. He pushed his mouth against mine, kissing me with an unstoppable intensity. He rose up on his knees, keeping my legs wrapped around his waist. He slowly lowered me until I was lying underneath him, never letting his mouth leave mine.

My skin flared with a pleasurable heat as his hands moved from my waist to trail up my sides, taking my shirt with it. He carefully removed it, leaving me with only my bikini on. He trailed kisses down my jawline and neck as he reached behind him to tug his own shirt off. I caught my breath at the sight of his body. It was built and rugged in a beautiful way that left my heart racing and desiring more.

He lowered his mouth to mine again, letting his lips part my own. I trailed my hands from his hair to his shoulder blades, where I gently tugged on him to bring him closer. My eyes shot open as I heard a snap.

His wings had burst out, and I stared at them in wonder. My reaction had him smiling at me as he leaned down to kiss my skin again. His soft touch guided my bikini straps down my shoulders before he reached beneath me to undo the whole thing. He quickly threw it aside, looking down at me as he did. I blushed and kept staring at his wings, letting the silky touch of them calm my nerves, which were growing by the minute.

He kissed on my neck, which made my eyes shut and my stomach do flips. He quickly threw his pants aside, exposing his bare bottom half to my pleading eyes. I shivered from the chill in the air. My body was no longer covered by anything except the thin layer of fabric that blocked the only thing keeping us from becoming one; however, he quickly removed that as well. After that, I no longer needed anything else to keep warm, because he lowered himself down the rest of the way, allowing us to be not two bodies, but one.

***

I laid there in his arms some time later with my eyes closed and a smile still plastered on my lips. I was facing him with my head resting on his pillow. He laid next to me, propping his head up with one hand while the other held me and softly rubbed up and down my bare back. His adoring eyes watched me, and his lips wore a warm smile.

I had never been happier in all my life, and I knew I could stay like this forever. Being in his arms. Being complete with him like we just were. To love someone and be loved by them in return was the best feeling in the world.

He leaned down to kiss me softly on the forehead. I felt giddy as he nuzzled my neck and whispered, "You have no idea how long I've wanted that."

I smiled at him as I reached my hand behind him to gently stroke his wings. They were still out, folded neatly behind his back in a lush, black curtain. I loved gazing at the glossy feathers and being able to touch their silky soft vanes. My eyes found his as I answered, "A long time, I'm going to guess."

He nodded with a grin. I closed my eyes, pressing my face against his bare chest. I yawned and mumbled, "Well, I hope it was everything that you dreamed it would be."

He chuckled against me. "No. It was so much better."

Feeling absolutely bubbly inside from head to toe, I smiled against his chest. It felt silly at how giddy he made me. With just a gentle caress of his warm hand or the hint of a smile at the corner of his lips, I found myself falling for him again and again. I didn't think that I could be any happier until he leaned down and whispered in my ear, "I love you, Raven."

My heart soared. Even though I now knew I was the girl he had fallen in love with, this was the first time he actually said the words 'I love you' directly to me. As a matter of fact, it was the first time anyone had said those words to me. I always fantasized about what it would sound and feel like when I heard those words for the first time, but this surge of warmth and euphoria was more than anything I could have expected.

I leaned back to look into his eyes. "I love you too, Kaden."

He laid his head down next to mine and pulled the blankets further up around us. His arms guided me closer to him, allowing his warmth to spread across my skin. I rested my head on his chest and said, "I wish it could be like this forever. I just want to stay here with you."

"Why don't you then?"

I looked up at him as he gazed down at me. I smiled and said, "I'm sure I can now. My dad-" I paused as my mind replayed the events that took place before the amazing night Kaden and I had shared. I still couldn't believe that my father had tossed me out the way he did.

Kaden sat up, gently bringing me with him. I clutched the sheet to my chest as he looked at me with concern embedded in his eyes. "What happened? Is he the reason I found you the way I did?"

I looked down and said, "Well, after I ran off to go back home, my dad freaked out on me. He thought I was my mom again, except this time-" I hesitated, looking back up at Kaden. He watched me with gentle eyes as he waited patiently for me to finish.

I swallowed and said, "This time he hit me and dragged me out of the house." Anger flooded Kaden's face, but I tried ignoring it as I continued, "He locked me out, so I was going to go through my window, but when I got there, Landon was waiting for me."

Kaden's body grew tense, and his features turned dark. His eyes narrowed into thin slits at the mention of Landon's name, and I could picture the gears turning in his head as he plotted ways to destroy Landon. Clearing my throat, I finished, "Landon was the reason I was on the ground outside my window."

"What did he do to you?" Kaden asked through gritted teeth.

My hand instinctively went up to rub my left cheek where Landon's fist had made its impact. I looked away from Kaden as I said, "He has a very good aim and a very strong punch."

Kaden gently removed my hand from my cheek and leaned down to kiss it. It was still a bit tender when he touched it, but I didn't mind. I would never mind if Kaden touched me. I would welcome his touch with open arms forever.

I smiled at him before letting it fall. I laid back down against the soft mattress and rolled over to face the wall. I didn't want Kaden to see the worry formulating on my face. Clenching my eyes shut, I whispered, "What if he comes after us again?" It took everything in me to keep my voice level.

Kaden eased down next to me and wrapped his arms around my midsection. He pressed his warm body against my back, and the feeling sent a wave of calmness and serenity through me. He kissed my shoulder and said, "I will always be there to protect you. Just don't ever trust them. If you come across one of them when I'm not with you, then find a way to get away from them as fast as you possibly can."

I nodded. If anything happened, Kaden could just set them on fire. They all feared him because of it, but they also knew the fire he possessed now was not as strong as what he'd once had. What if they used that against him?

I looked at him over my shoulder and asked, "What if they bind your hands, Kaden? You said you have to open and close your fists to create fire. What if they bind your hands to where you can't do that?"

"Shh," he hushed, leaning down to kiss me softly. My lips parted as his tongue brushed past them, and he kissed me with a tenderness that made my heart melt. When he pulled back, I gave him a small smile. He grinned back at me and said, "Get some sleep, little birdie. It's late."

I giggled - the nickname recalled happy memories for me. When I was little, the voice in the wind from my clearing would always call me little birdy because my name was Raven. It was his very own nickname for me. This was just more proof that everything he said was true. He'd been there then, and he was here now. He was mine, and I was his.

I smiled and let my head fall against the pillow once more. Sleep quickly overtook me, and I had never slept better in all of my life.

Chapter Twenty-One

MY EYES SLOWLY FLUTTERED open, and I blinked a couple of times as I started to wake up. Looking next to me, I found Kaden lying there with his arm still draped around me. Strands of his dark hair had fallen across his face as he slept, and the edges of his hair stood up slightly in a cute way. His eyes were still shut, and he was breathing softly. I couldn't contain my smile as I watched him. He looked so incredible, and I still had trouble believing that he was all mine.

My upbeat spirit had my entire body buzzing with warmth as I slowly slid out from underneath his arm to get out of bed. I looked back at him to make sure he was still asleep. I didn't want to wake him. He needed to rest too.

When I was satisfied that he was still sleeping, I walked into the bathroom and closed the door as much as I could with it still broken. I should probably offer to fix that. I started the shower, letting it get warm before stepping into its warm embrace.

The heat of the water sent goosebumps up and down my arms as I tilted my face up towards the raining drops. Memories of last night were flashing through my mind in a blissful succession. I couldn't stop grinning as I remembered the feel of his hands touching every part of me, and the way his lips had kissed me with a long felt desire.

I was so caught up in my thoughts that I didn't notice Kaden come in. When I felt arms encircle me from behind, my heart sped up. My eyes shot open, and I jumped, which caused Kaden to chuckle behind me. He pressed my back against him in a reassuring hold as he kissed on my neck and shoulder.

"Good morning," he said as he turned me to face him.

I smiled at him while reaching my arms up to wrap them around his neck. I kissed him once and said, "Good morning."

One kiss wasn't enough for him though because he plunged his hands into my hair, bringing my lips to his. The intensity of the kiss mirrored last night as his soft lips and tongue begged for me. He grabbed me under my bottom and lifted me up, guiding my legs to wrap around his waist. Turning quickly, he pinned me inbetween the shower wall and his warm body. He trailed kisses along my neck as my eyes shut, and my head tilted back. His hands grabbed at my hips and gently slid me lower onto him, letting us unite once more.

***

"I think I'm going to try to go to work today," I said as I

finished slipping on my shirt. Kaden stood there, taking in the sight of me getting dressed. He only wore his boxers and jeans, and he held his shirt in his hands. Once I was dressed, he gave me one last heated gaze before tugging his shirt on over his head.

"Are you sure?" he asked. He walked over to me and pulled me into his arms. "You aren't still hurting from everything?"

I laughed and placed my hand on his chest as I grumbled, "I'm fine. It just feels odd not working or doing anything. Besides, if I can manage to do what we did last night and just a few minutes ago, I think I can handle being a cashier."

His cheeks grew rosier as a smile lit up his face. My heart leapt at the sight of him blushing, and he tried to hide his colored cheeks by kissing me softly. When he pulled back the rosiness had died down some, and he cleared his throat.

When his eyes were able to meet mine again, he said, "I was being careful. If you thought last night and this morning was something, just wait until you're fully recovered."

I blushed a bright red crimson and stepped back from him, giggling. I took his hand and said, "All right Romeo. I'll take your word for it. Will you walk me to the bookstore now?"

He brought my hand up to his mouth and brushed his soft lips across the skin. I smiled at him as he looked at me with a twinkle in his eye. He seemed so happy now, more so than I had ever seen him.

He hugged me and said, "Of course."

We started off towards town, talking and laughing the whole way. Not only was Kaden noticeably happier and less stressed, but I was too. I was in such high spirits due to the relief that came with finally knowing the truth about everything, and it felt good to know that Kaden and I were able to be together. I was hopeful that from now on, we could start building a real life and relationship with one another.

He meant so much to me, and the more he talked, the more I felt like I truly had known him for so long. He'd been there my whole life, hiding in the shadows. He'd always been watching from afar, but now he was here with me. He'd given up everything he knew for me, and I would cherish that forever. I hoped that one day I could repay him for all he had done for me.

"So what are you going to do while I'm here working?" I asked as we walked along the sidewalk through town.

He looked down at me and squeezed my hand. "Well, I was thinking if you really wanted to stay with me after what happened with your dad, I would go to your house to get your stuff. I'll just get the stuff you really want for now. All the stuff you actually use or care about."

I mulled over the idea of actually living with Kaden. Graduation was coming up, and I had been planning on leaving home for college anyways. I couldn't watch over my dad forever. I had to live for myself at some point. This could be a good test run to see how he did on his own before I *actually* left.

Flashing him a wide grin, I nodded. "That would be nice. And I'm sure you would know what stuff to get, considering you watched me grow up."

That was still so crazy to think about. He had seen so much of me and my life. I wondered if he could remember parts that even I couldn't anymore. I wondered if he remembered my mom.

His smile deepened, and he dipped his head down in a slight nod. "And I won't be far obviously. As soon as I have your stuff moved, I'm coming back to the store. I don't want us separating too much right now. Not until I've been able to deal with the others."

I didn't want to think about another possible attack so soon, but I knew there was a chance of one. As long as Landon and the other's were around, there was always going to be a chance of danger. Even so, as long as Kaden and I had each other, I felt like we could overcome anything, even a group of malicious fallen angels. Hopefully though, we wouldn't need to.

When we made it to the bookstore, I could see Mrs. Morea inside behind the counter as she sorted the magazines. At first, I was afraid she was going to be mad that I hadn't been there, but then I remembered Kaden made her believe she gave me the time off. There was still a chance that it hadn't worked though, which would mean I was going to be in for it.

Turning back to meet Kaden's eyes, I leaned in and kissed him softly. "I love you."

He pulled me into a tight embrace. "I love you too, Raven."

I flashed him another smile before turning to make my

way inside the store. The bell over the door chimed when I entered. Mrs. Morea looked up from her stack of magazines, staring at me in surprise.

"Raven? I thought I gave you this week off?" She scratched at her head, puzzled. "Are you here to buy something?" After she took me in for another moment, her eyes grew wide, and her chin dropped slightly. "Why are you all bruised and bandaged on your face?"

I smiled to myself. Not only had Kaden's little dream adventures worked, but Mrs. Morea actually seemed genuinely concerned about my wellbeing. That in itself made me thoroughly happy.

"I'm fine, Mrs. Morea. I appreciate the time off too, but I felt like coming to work anyways. Why don't you go and be with your granddaughter? I'm sure you would much rather be visiting her than stuck here working. How is she doing?"

She stared at me in awe. I wasn't quite sure what I'd done, but she slowly answered, "She's good. Thank you for asking." She blinked a few more times, reminding me of a person who was stuck in a trance.

Clearing her throat, she finally reached for her purse. "I think you're right. I'll go see them. You may take over tonight."

I smiled and got behind the counter as she approached the front door. Before she walked out, she stopped and turned around to look at me. "Raven, I just wanted to say that I'm sorry for all the awful things I've said to you over the years. You really are a fantastic worker, and I appreciate all the work that you've done for me."

She lifted her purse higher onto her shoulder and grabbed the doorknob. Glancing another apologetic look at me, she said one last time, "Again, I'm very sorry." With that, she turned the knob and walked out.

I stared at the spot where she had been standing in disbelief. Had Mrs. Morea just apologized to me? She had never shown any sort of remorse or kindness towards me before. She was a callous old woman, so I had no idea what had sparked this sudden change in her.

As I thought more about it, I was beginning to piece together the possibility that Kaden had convinced Mrs. Morea of more than just giving me the week off. He might have forced her to face the way she'd treated me in the past, which had resulted in her feeling compelled to apologize. He hadn't had to do that of course, and I still wasn't positive that it had been him. Still, it was starting to amaze me how much care Kaden put into matters concerning me.

Once I was alone, I organized the rest of the magazines. I walked to the stand in front of the counter with my back to the door, and I began setting the magazines out. As I worked to place them in an organized fashion, the bell above the door chimed.

I turned around and smiled at the customer, but the more I looked at him, the more my smile began to fade. It was a lean guy who wore a black t-shirt with a light scarf. Purple eyeliner traced his smiling eyes, and his blue hair was styled to the side. It was the hair that caught my attention. It seemed very familiar. Where had I seen someone with blue hair though?

Then it hit me, and the world began to tilt beneath my feet. I held my breath as his menacing grin teased me. He was one of Landon's men, the one Kaden called Malachi. My smile fell the rest of the way, and I turned to rush behind the counter in an attempt to get as far away as I could.

Malachi laughed and said, "I would be running to the door if I were you. I believe we have something very important to you at the church."

I stopped dead in my tracks. My lip quivered as I swallowed the lump in my throat and turned to face Malachi. He was leaning against the counter, smirking at me. My heart fell at the implied meaning of his words. "What do you mean?"

His grin broadened at me as he said, "You didn't show up like Landon thought you would, so he had to push you into coming. We have your precious angel at the church, and I don't know how much longer Landon is going to wait before he kills him."

Tears welled in my eyes, and my knees buckled. I caught myself on the wall and clenched my eyes shut. They had Kaden. I couldn't let anything happen to him, but what if this was a trick? Kaden said not to trust them, but then again, what if it wasn't a trick? What if they really did have him? This was my chance to protect and save him, as he had always done for me.

I narrowed my eyes at Malachi and asked, "How do I know you're telling the truth?"

He leaned closer and said, "You don't. But are you willing to risk that?"

He was right. I wasn't willing to risk it. I sped past the counter and him, rushing out the door and into the crowd of people outside. My eyes frantically scanned the space around me. I didn't know where or how far away the abandoned church was. How was I supposed to get there in time?

Malachi came up behind me and grabbed my wrist, not trying to be gentle at all. He pulled me along with him, running past the people and buildings. I stumbled a few times as I fought to keep up with him, but I refused to let myself fall. I had to get to Kaden.

When we neared the edge of town and were away from any prying eyes, he didn't slow down. His wings, a matted black, shot out from his back. My heart caught in my throat, and my fear mounted as they beat the air, raising us up into it.

As his feathered wings lifted us up into the sky, he continued to grip my wrist tightly. My feet left the ground as we went higher, and Malachi laughed wickedly as he dangled me above the faraway land. My breath came out quickly as I held onto his arm, and pain shot up my side. He was holding my right wrist, which was pulling on my side where Chesed had stabbed me. The skin and surrounding area was burning, and I thought I was going to pass out from the swelling fire I felt on the wound. Luckily, the adrenaline from flying and being frightened was keeping me very much conscious.

My dark hair whipped around in the brisk air as I looked up at Malachi, who was staring ahead with the look of a madman. His eyes were opened wide in an animalistic stare, and his mouth was curled up in a sneering grin. The sight of him sent chills down my spine.

I held onto his wrist with both hands in an attempt to keep from falling as I looked down below me. We were insanely high, and the trees were just small brown specks below us. I clenched my eyes shut and looked back up. Looking down was a big mistake.

I opened my eyes to stare ahead, and my heart soared when I saw the church coming into view. Malachi was beginning to lower us closer to the ground, and nerves buzzed beneath my skin.

I'm coming Kaden! Just hold on!

When we were in front of the church, Malachi stopped moving forward. He continued to dangle me in the air, so I looked down. I was still nearly ten feet above the ground. My eyes shot back up to Malachi who laughed darkly into my horrified eyes. He blew me a kiss before letting go of me. I grabbed at the air as I fell towards the ground. My stomach was in my throat, and I felt like I was falling in slow motion. Malachi hovered above me, smiling the whole time I fell.

My body finally collided with the ground, and I landed hard on my side with a loud crack. The wind left me, and I laid there, unable to move from the shock of the fall. My mind was disoriented, but as soon as I gathered myself, my body registered the damage of the impact. An incredible pain flared up in my left arm, which was pinned between my body and the ground. I wailed through gritted teeth as the realization hit me that my arm was broken. A searing burn was rocketing through me, and I had to roll to the side as my stomach lurched and I threw up.

"Ugh," Malachi spat as he hovered above me. "That is seriously disgusting."

He landed next to me as I finished emptying my stomach. Before I knew what he was doing, he grabbed my ankle and started dragging me towards the front doors of the church. I clawed at the grass with my right hand, trying to stop him from pulling me, but the rocks and sticks on the ground were cutting up my stomach the further along he went.

I looked around frantically, searching for something to use as a weapon. I spotted a large rock, and I fumbled at it as we went. My fingers dug into the dirt and grass as I struggled to grip the stone. I yanked it from the ground as I was forced past it, and dirt went flying into my face. I ignored it as I panted and turned just enough to throw it at the back of Malachi's head. The rock smashed into his blue hair, and I was happy to see the impact made him stumble and fall.

When he dropped to his knees, I swung my leg, kicking him as hard as I could in the face. That sent him backwards, and he collapsed onto his back. I quickly took my chance and stood up. Wanting desperately to get to Kaden, I raced for the doors of the church.

I looked back over my shoulder at Malachi who was sitting up and clutching his bleeding face. He glared at me and yelled "You bitch! You'll pay for that!"

Looking forward again, I shoved the doors to the massive structure open. Running in, I screamed Kaden's name. I looked around the furnitureless sanctuary for him, but I only saw the group of fallen angels who had kidnapped me before. Landon stood at the front of them, grinning at me. The ones behind him were glaring in my direction. Some of them still had healing burns from that night.

Struggling to catch my breath after running and fighting with Malachi, I finally managed to take in a gulp of air. I glared at Landon and screamed, "Where is he? Where's Kaden?"

At that same moment, Malachi came back up behind me and grabbed me around the arms. He pinned them to my sides, which made me scream out in agony as his arm tightened around my left one. The pain was so excruciating that I could no longer stand on my own legs. The only thing holding me up was Malachi.

My feet dragged across the stone floor as Malachi approached Landon who reached out and cupped my chin in a tight grip. My eyes were half shut as I looked at him with endless pain soaring through me. Landon glanced down at my left arm, raising his brow as he took in the already bruising skin and oddly angled shape of it.

Landon found my eyes again as he grinned darkly. "Did something happen to your arm?" He reached out to touch it, and when I winced, he gave me an evil smirk. He grabbed it and squeezed hard.

An agonizing wail racked my body as the pain became indescribable. I could feel the urge to vomit rising up in me again as pulses of pressure shot up my arm. If I did get sick, I just hoped it would go all over the monster in front of me.

"That's right. Scream." His grip was letting up on my arm, and as he let go, my mind clouded. I was growing dizzy from all of the pain.

He stepped back from me and looked at Chesed, who stood to his right. "Have everyone go outside. Wait for Kaden to come, and when he gets here, ambush him. Make sure his hands are bound. I don't want him using his fire again."

My eyes started to slip closed, but I couldn't let them. They were going to hurt Kaden.

"No. Stop. Please, don't hurt him," I said through heavy breaths. I tried wiggling in Malachi's grip, but it sent another jolt of pain through me. I slumped forward in his arms, and I was sure I was going to throw up.

Landon grabbed my hair and yanked on it to force me to look up at him. All the men who'd been behind him were gone, which meant they were outside waiting on Kaden. Tears were starting to flow from my eyes as I glared at Landon, asking, "Kaden isn't here?"

"Why no, he isn't, I'm afraid." Landon grinned at me as he ran his free hand down my cheek. His touch repulsed me, and I tried pulling back from it. He held me in place by my hair as he continued, "He will be soon though. Now that we have you, the bait. You see, without you, Kaden wouldn't come to us again, because he wouldn't want to risk your life, so I had to take you in order to persuade him to come here.

"When he realizes I have you, he will come in hopes of getting you back, but my men will be ready. After we have him bound, we will make him suffer by killing you slowly in front of him. Don't worry though. We will kill him shortly afterwards."

I closed my eyes as his words dug into me. I was the bait that would lead to Kaden's death. I shouldn't have believed Malachi. I should've listened to Kaden's warning: *do not trust any of them*. I was stupid though, and I fell for their trick. Now Kaden and I were both going to die.

Angry tears streamed down my cheeks as I glared at Landon. I couldn't let myself believe they would win. Kaden was stronger than all of them. Kaden was good, and good always triumphs over evil. We would find a way out of this.

"Please," I pleaded with Landon, "Don't hurt him."

He grinned and looked at Malachi. "What do you think? Should I let Kaden live, Malachi?"

He chuckled against me and said, "No way. And she deserves to suffer just as much as that sorry excuse for a fallen angel. Look what she did to my face!" He squeezed me tighter as he added, "Her knowing that Kaden will die is the perfect punishment to go alongside all the physical pain we will cause her."

As his grip grew tighter against my left arm, another wail escaped me. A wave of nausea hit me, and my body slumped forward again. My breaths were coming out quick and heavy, and my vision was starting to get fuzzy at the corners. When I was able to control my breathing and focus again, all three of us looked up as the sound of wings came from outside, followed by the sound of rising voices and commotion.

Landon smiled wickedly at me as he said, "It sounds like it's almost time for the show to start."

Chapter Twenty-Two

CRYING HYSTERICALLY, I SQUIRMED in Malachi's arms again. I couldn't let them get a hold of Kaden. I couldn't let them hurt him. Malachi held me firmly in place, not letting me escape. He turned us around to where we faced the door, and Landon came to stand to my left. We watched the entryway, and my heart raced as I thought of what would happen when those doors opened.

When one of the wooden frames was flung open, my heart soared in hopes that it was Kaden, fully intact, but it was only one of the fallen angels. I recognized him as the one who had choked me with a rope the last time I was here. His black wings had feathers missing, and blood seeped from open wounds along his body. Burns covered his arms and stomach in raised, bubbling patches. He looked terrible as he panted and looked at Landon.

Landon glared at him and clenched his jaw. He inhaled deeply to calm the annoyance that was displayed across his features. "What happened? Why are you in here and not out there, Bronc?"

Bronc continued panting as he struggled to answer. "Kaden is winning. He's too fast and too strong. We weren't able to catch him off guard enough to bind his hands."

I looked at Landon, and hope swelled within me. He glared at me as I gave him a confident, bitter smile. "See," I said with venom lacing each word. "You cannot defeat him. Kaden will always win. There is nothing you can do to stop him."

Landon looked back towards Bronc, listening to the fighting still raging outside. Yells and screams of pain flooded into the church as he debated what to do. Finally, he sneered at me. Turning his attention back to Bronc, he said, "You need a distraction? I'll give you a distraction."

Seeming to know what was about to happen, Bronc backed away. He left to join the fight back outside as Landon looked at me. He had a horrifying expression of pure rage on his face. His eyes were ablaze, and they glared down at me. His tight mouth was turned down at the corners, and he took angry breaths.

He grabbed me around the neck, squeezing hard, and Malachi's arms left me. I used my right hand to try and pull Landon's hand away from my throat, but he held it too tightly for my damaged body to do anything. My air was being cut off as he dangled me above the floor, and he walked with purpose towards the doors of the church.

When he stepped outside, I could barely see past the growing fog that clouded my vision in order to gauge what was happening. All I could manage to see was the way Kaden moved, throwing fire and punches at all his opponents. He wore an angry expression as he fought anyone who dared come close to him. I wanted to smile, seeing how Kaden was undefeatable, but I was quickly growing limp from lack of air.

"Kaden!" Landon yelled.

I watched with half closed eyes as Kaden looked towards us. As soon as he saw me dangling above the ground and with Landon's tight grip squeezed around my throat, his face fell. His looking away from the fight and seeing me was all the guys needed. They pounced on Kaden all at once, and I could no longer see him. He was buried beneath all of the fallen angels as they worked to bind his hands behind his back.

Landon let go of me then, and I collapsed to the ground in a crumpled heap, inhaling as much air as I possibly could. I panted, unable to do anything except reach for oxygen to fill my lungs again. My head was spinning as the world seemed to tilt and sway underneath me, and my limbs had no energy to them. When I tried standing, I only fell back down. My surroundings were hazy around me, and I thought I was going to pass out.

"Oh no you don't," Landon said.

He reached down and picked me up by my hair. Dragging me back inside of the church, he brought us to where Malachi waited. Landon let go of my hair, and Malachi reached down to jerk me up. He gripped me tightly around my arms, causing pain to soar up my body again. I moaned through clenched teeth while taking steady breaths in an attempt to keep the rising bile at bay. His arms remained firm around me to keep me from moving or escaping.

I watched in horror as all the other fallen angels came back inside. Four of them held Kaden, who was jerking around and trying to wiggle his way out of their hold. His hands were behind his back, bound in cloth, which prevented him from being able to make fire. This sent a wave of panic through me, but I didn't let it shake me. I refused to give up without a fight.

Two men closed the doors behind them as everyone made it into the center of the room. Kaden was watching me with pain and worry in his eyes. His eyes flicked to my left in Landon's direction, and fury spread across Kaden's features. He pushed and pulled against the four men again in an angry attempt to get to Landon. The four men began to struggle with their hold, and another angel had to step in to help restrain him.

Landon chuckled and took a step forward as the five men brought Kaden to his knees. Kaden was breathing hard, anger visibly building and coursing through him. I looked around the room at the rest of the fallen angels. They all looked like they had been through Hell. Each of them was bleeding and had burns painting their bodies. Kaden had really delivered some damage, but it still wasn't enough.

Looking back at him, I realized he only had a few cuts on his bare torso and arms. Even though he'd taken the least amount of beating, tears still poured down my cheeks. I didn't want anyone to hurt him, and I didn't want us to die this way. Landon and his men could not win.

"Well, well, well. Kaden," Landon said, taking slow, measured steps towards him. "So nice of you to join us. You know, we all feel a bit rejected since you just walked out on us. Especially after we took you in the way we did."

Kaden glared at him and said, "I was never one of you."

Landon rolled his eyes and began walking back towards me. "Yes, yes. We all know. You were weak, and that weakness let you fall in love with a human all over again."

Landon stopped right in front of me, waving his hand at Malachi. Malachi let me go and stepped back from me. I stood there with my legs wobbling beneath me, and I fought the urge to drop to my knees. That would be like admitting defeat, which was something I wouldn't do. Not to a monster like him.

Landon stepped aside, letting Kaden's eyes fall on me. His face changed from anger to anguish. "See," Landon said as he watched Kaden's face change. "Weakness. She is your weakness, and that will be how we make you pay. No one walks out on us."

Before I had a chance to react or even know what was coming, Landon backhanded me, sending me to the floor. I landed hard on my left arm, and as soon as my arm cracked against the ground, a piercing cry echoed out from my body and around the room. I rolled onto my back, clenching my eyes shut as I held my shattered left arm.

"Do not touch her!" Kaden screamed.

I rolled my head to the side to look at him. His wide eyes frantically searched me as a picture of misery flooded his features. His whole body jerked around as he struggled to fight through their hold. He was trying so hard to fight them off, but five against one was too much.

Trying to pull strength into my body, I closed my eyes. Using my right arm to push myself to a sitting position, I started to rise up. Landon chuckled and said, "Malachi. Would you like to repay Raven for what she did to you?"

I looked up at Malachi, who gave me an evil smile. "It would be my pleasure."

I knew what was coming, so I tried pushing myself up quicker to make a run for it. Malachi was too fast though. He pulled his leg back then swung it at me. His foot smashed into my face with a loud crack.

A pained cry erupted from my mouth as I collapsed onto my back. Blood poured from my nose, which now bent under my touch. I clutched my face as the taste of blood and sweat mixed in my mouth. Kaden panted and struggled in the grips of his captors as I fought to gather my bearings. I tried to lift my head up, but I was quickly losing strength.

I laid there as Landon came to stand above me. He was smiling down at me, so I decided to take my chance. I pulled every bit of strength I had in me and quickly brought my foot up to kick him hard in between the legs. He doubled over in pain, so I pushed myself to my feet and limped towards Kaden. I could only make it a step before Bronc was on me, wrapping his beloved rope around my neck and pulling me back.

He tugged hard, and I choked as my air was cut off. Kaden looked at me with horror in his eyes. Bronc responded to his panic by pulling harder. I involuntarily let out a strained gurgle as I used my right hand to try to claw at the rope, but it was pointless. Kaden pulled at the men holding him back again, and one of them lost their grip. Kaden started to get up in an attempt to reach me, but two more men quickly joined in holding him back.

"Landon!" Kaden yelled, "Stop hurting her! You don't need to do this. She didn't do anything!"

Landon held up his hand toward Bronc, signaling for him to stop. He ceased choking me, and I coughed as I took in deep breaths of air. I didn't have time to rejoice over the fact that I could breathe again though, because Bronc continued to hold onto me. He wasn't letting me go anywhere.

Landon glared at Kaden as he approached him. He got down in Kaden's face as he spat, "She didn't do anything? She did everything! She is the reason you fell, Kaden. She is the reason that you left the group. She is the reason half my men got burned from your flames. She is the reason that both of you are here now, about to die."

My eyes slipped closed, and my lip quivered as tears streamed down my cheeks. Landon was crazy. This was all because he and his men couldn't let Kaden go. Their thirst for blood and revenge outweighed everything.

Even so, a small part of me felt guilty for what was going on. I had fallen for their trap even after being warned. Granted, all I wanted was for Kaden and I to be able to stay together and build a normal life, but none of that seemed possible now. I had endangered us both.

"Raven," Kaden said softly. My eyes fluttered open as

my gaze found his. His brow was furrowed in sorrow and worry. "This isn't your fault."

Landon grew angry at this. "Do not lie to her anymore, Kaden!" Landon reached his arm high then brought it down, backhanding Kaden hard across the face.

The sound of Landon hitting Kaden made my heart break, and I cried harder, screaming, "Don't please! Please don't hurt him! You say it's my fault, right? So leave him alone! Fight me! Punish me! Just leave him out of it!"

"Raven, no!" Kaden said, looking at me with pain written across his face, only it wasn't from the slap that Landon delivered.

He didn't want me hurt, just as I didn't want him in pain or danger. But I would do whatever I had to to keep him safe. He had defined me as brave before, and to me, this was the moment where I actually felt brave. I could be strong and courageous if it meant protecting the one I loved.

Landon smiled and took a step towards me. Kaden's face scrunched up in anger again as he roared at Landon, "If you touch her, I swear I will end your life, you sick bastard!"

Landon looked back at Kaden as he stood next to me. He wore a large grin as he taunted, "Oh, what? You mean like this?"

Landon backhanded me again. I clenched my eyes shut against the pain, but I refused to cry out. I wanted to put up as much of a fight as I could. Kaden jerked forward again in a desperate attempt to get past those holding him back. Landon laughed at Kaden's struggle. My anger was starting to swell too. I would not let him do this.

I threw my head back against Bronc, and he grunted as the back of my head smashed into his face. His grip loosened enough for me to slip away, so I ran at Landon. Tackling him hard, I threw us both to the floor. He watched me with a dumbfounded expression as he worked to piece together what had just happened. He was too slow though. I landed on top of him and reared my right arm back to punch him hard in the face.

That was all I had time to do because he quickly recovered and swung at me too, knocking me sideways. Bronc and Malachi grabbed me on both sides, and they yanked me up. Landon swayed slightly as he got to his feet, touching his now bleeding nose. I smiled triumphantly at him, knowing that if I died, I had at least made him bleed too.

My eyes found Kaden who gave me a small smile. He was proud of me. I wanted him to be proud of me. His smile quickly faded though, because Landon stormed over to me. I glared at him as he punched me hard in the abdomen. The breath left me, and I doubled over in pain. Bronc and Malachi pulled me up straight again, letting Landon throw another punch at my face. My broken nose had gone slightly numb by this point, but Landon resurfaced the pain along with busting my lip. I gagged as I was forced to spit up blood, and my vision grew blurry.

I closed my eyes, trying to blink away the pain. I could faintly hear Kaden yelling and struggling again, but it was hard to focus on the sound. My body was starting to give up at this point. It took a lot just to open my eyes again. My legs were now too weak to stand, but Malachi and Bronc held me up. I slumped forward, unable to even keep my head up anymore. Malachi grabbed me by the hair and forced my face to tilt up in order to see Landon.

He stood several feet away from me by Kaden. Landon gave one pleased look at his worry-stricken face and said, "I hope you enjoyed the show, Kaden. I think it's time for the grand finale though."

Kaden looked back and forth from Landon to me with wide and horrified eyes, and his brow was furrowed in anguish. A deep frown masked his lips as his face grew pale. Landon pulled a gun out of his back pocket and aimed it right at me. A tear rolled down my cheek as I looked at Kaden. I wanted him to be the last thing I saw.

I watched as Kaden fought harder than he had the whole time to get away. Those holding him were struggling again. Time seemed to stop as he leaned forward, and his dark wings shot out from his back. He looked at me, as he flapped them hard. This gust of movement propelled him forward and sent him flying out of their grasp. He flew towards me, faster than he had ever flown before. Landon fired the gun at the same moment, but before it could hit me, Kaden jumped in the way.

Chapter Twenty-Three

MY BODY FROZE, AND the scream I wanted to let out got strangled in my throat. Kaden's expanse of black wings fell across my eyes, blocking my view as the bullet should have collided with him, but right when it would have hit, a bright, white light filled the entire room.

The light was blinding, so I was forced to close my eyes. The hands that had been holding me let go, no doubt trying to hide their eyes from the blinding light as well. Without their support, I collapsed to the ground. I remained in a broken heap as I waited for the light to disappear.

When it began to recede, I was able to slowly open my eyes once more. My jaw dropped when I saw the source of the light. Lining the walls of the room were dozens upon dozens of angels. Each and every one of them had glistening white wings upon their backs, and they wore loose, white clothing. The angels were of different sizes, colors, and builds, yet each was more beautiful than the last.

As the light continued to fade towards the center of the room, an angel stepped forward from where he stood against the wall. He had wavy blond hair that was tied back with a white ribbon at the base of his neck, and his large, frost-colored wings were folded behind him. His eyes were a beautiful silver, and his skin was a stunning alabaster. He was beautiful, and even though he was smaller than some of the other angels, the sheer power that emanated from him was greater than any other in the room.

He was stunning yet terrifying.

I watched as this magnificent angel approached where the light was still glowing in the form of another angel. The glow was right where Kaden had been standing, and as the light disappeared altogether, the group of fallen angels let out a chorus of gasps. My eyes grew wide as I stared up in wonder at Kaden.

His wings were no longer the black that reflected the night sky. They now matched the rest of the angel's wings that surrounded us. They were a luminescent white, matching the loose fitting pants that he was now wearing. All of the cuts had disappeared from his body, and his skin now had a slight shimmer to it.

"Impossible," Landon whispered.

The blond angel who approached Kaden turned to face the group of fallen angels. Each one of them, fearing the newly arrived guests, fled out of the church doors. The blond angel turned towards the angels surrounding the room, signaling to each of them. They nodded before flying after the fallen angels. After that, there was just me, Kaden, this man, and one last angel.

Kaden turned. His eyes found my broken and bloody body, still lying on the floor. He hurriedly knelt down and scooped me onto his lap, clutching me to him. Tears flooded his eyes as he looked towards the female angel, who stood a few feet away.

"Ivee, please heal her! I beg you!"

The female angel looked towards the other, who nodded his approval. Ivee walked towards me then. Her hair was a brilliant silver that flowed all the way down to the floor, and her tight dress matched her beautiful hair. Her eyes were a bit unnerving though, as they were red and slitted like a serpent.

I clutched to Kaden tighter as she knelt down next to me. She smiled as though to reassure me that I was safe before placing her hand on my heart. She closed her eyes as a small glow lit beneath her hand. I closed my eyes too as an incredible lightness overtook me. I felt peace and love and security, feelings I had come to associate with Kaden and his presence.

I opened my eyes as Ivee's hand fell away from me. She looked at Kaden and said in a honey sweet voice, "She is healed."

She was right. I didn't feel pain anywhere anymore. I lifted my left arm, which I could move now. I touched my cheek, nose, and entire body, not feeling any sort of pain. I even lifted up the bottom of my shirt to see that the wound where Chesed stabbed me was now gone too.

I looked up at Kaden, and he smiled brightly into my

eyes, relief and joy spreading across his face. He brushed my hair away from my forehead as he explained, "Ivee is an angel with the ability to heal. That's a very rare trait among angels."

I smiled at him as relief washed over my entire body. Tears rolled down my cheeks as I flung my arms around his neck, hugging him tightly. He held me just as close, with his face buried in my hair. I pulled back from him, looking into his eyes. They stared back into mine with nothing but love.

"I-" I choked, "I thought I lost you."

Kaden's gentle touch caressed my cheek as he smiled down at me. "You will never lose me." He looked at the male angel who was watching us. "Only I'm not exactly sure what happened. Gabriel?"

Gabriel smiled at us, and he reached his hand down to help me up. I looked at Kaden, who nodded to me, letting me know it was safe. I looked back at Gabriel, accepting his hand. He helped me to my feet, and Kaden quickly stood too. Kaden looked at his wings over his shoulder then back to Gabriel.

"How did this happen?" Kaden asked in awe. "I didn't know that fallen angels could become angelic again."

Gabriel smiled and said, "That's because before this, a fallen angel has never been able to love after falling. You are the first fallen to turn back into an angel." Gabriel looked at me with a warm smile before turning his silver eyes back to Kaden. "Kaden, your love for Raven kept you from filling with hatred, even after being cast out. When you were willing to sacrifice yourself for her because of your love for her, God granted you back your angelic abilities."

Gabriel looked at me and added, "God is a sucker for love." Looking back to Kaden, he finished, "No fallen angel has ever been able to make a sacrifice in the name of love."

Smiling from ear to ear, Kaden looked at me. He grabbed me around the waist and twirled me around, laughing. "I'm an angel again!

He flew us up into the air, and my heart soared. It felt so good to laugh with him again, something I was sure had been lost forever just a few moments ago.

Gabriel cleared his throat, bringing our attention back to him. Kaden sheepishly lowered us down to face Gabriel again who said, "You aren't an angel yet. He granted you your angelic state to show you one option."

Kaden glanced at me then back at Gabriel. "Option?"

Ivee, who had been standing to the side of Gabriel, stepped forward. A warm look passed between her and Gabriel as they smiled at each other. Ivee turned her attention to us as she explained, "Yes. Option. You must choose. You may either come back to Heaven to reclaim your job as a guardian angel." She gestured to Kaden and how he appeared now with white wings. Her red eyes flicked in my direction as she continued, "Or you may remain here on Earth with Raven."

I looked at Kaden as my heart sunk. I thought we were going to be able to be together, but now that I realized what he could have instead, I wouldn't let him choose me. The whole time we had been together, he'd always hated himself for being fallen. I knew being an angel again would mean the world to him. As much as my heart broke when I thought about him leaving me, I knew he had to choose being an angel again. That's who he was.

Wrapping my arms around his warm body one last time, I looked into his eyes, and my own filled with fresh tears. "Kaden, you hate being a fallen angel. This is your chance to go back and be happy. You should choose to be an angel again. That's what you've been wanting this whole time."

He pulled me close to him, hugging his arms around my lower back. He stared down into my eyes as he processed my words. Slowly, he nodded. "You're right. I have missed being an angel. I've missed it a lot actually, and it would be nice to be one again."

Looking down, I pressed my face into his chest as more tears flowed from me. I knew I shouldn't be crying. I should feel happy for him, but it was so hard when I knew this was it. This was going to be goodbye.

He pulled back slightly and used his finger to tilt my face up to look into his eyes. He kissed me softly then pulled back. "But as much as I miss being an angel, I'd miss you a thousand times more. You're right when you say that being an angel makes me happy, but you, Raven, you make me feel *alive*. You make me feel amazed, thrilled, and loved all combined into one big emotion that I can barely contain. I fell for you once, and if I went back, I promise you that I would just fall again. I will always choose you."

I squeezed my eyes shut as I smiled through the tears. I couldn't stop them from flowing, but they were no longer from the ache in my chest. They were from pure and utter joy.

Kaden pulled me close, resting my head against his chest as he looked at Gabriel and Ivee. He tilted his chin up slightly and said with determination, "I choose Raven."

Gabriel smiled and said, "We thought that's what you would choose. You may remain on earth with Raven. Your wings and abilities will remain as they were when you were fallen. Well, almost at least. The wings will have a small alteration."

Gabriel waved his hand in front of Kaden, enveloping him in a bright light again. I had to step back and shield my eyes until the light was gone. Once it disappeared, Kaden stood before me in the jeans that he had been wearing before. The only difference now was his wings.

Instead of being black or white, they were a stunning silver, shining much like the stars that I felt so close to when Kaden and I flew together at night. They shimmered and caught the light in a crystal-like shine. My jaw dropped at their beauty, and I stepped forward to brush my fingers through the silky feathers. Kaden smiled down at me after looking at them.

"Do you like them?" he asked, circling his arms around me once more.

I nodded, smiling up at him. "They're perfect. Better than the white or black. Do you like them?"

He grinned and leaned his forehead against mine. "I love them."

We both looked at Ivee as she explained, "They're silver,

representing that you were once angel and once fallen. Now you are a mix of both, filled with love and goodness while still inhabiting Earth without being expected to return to Heaven."

Kaden smiled at the two angels and held his hand out for them to shake in thanks. They each shook it with a smile as Kaden said, "Thank you, both of you. For everything."

Gabriel and Ivee each nodded before being swallowed up in light. When the light disappeared, they were gone. I looked back at Kaden, who stared down at me with an incredible smile. He pulled me further against him and whispered, "Are you ready to go home?"

I looked at the doors. "What about Landon and everyone else?"

Kaden's wings beat the air, bringing us up and out of the church. He held me close, never once making me afraid of falling. I glanced over his shoulder at his new wings. The setting sun cast a glow upon them, and each feather shined in the light. It looked as though small stars were sprinkled across them. They were the most mesmerizing thing I had ever seen.

He leaned close to my ear as we flew through the cool breeze. "The other angels will have handled Landon and the rest of them. I just wish I could have had a chance to help rid the world of Landon too."

"I'm just glad he's gone," I said, smiling warmly in the pale orange of the fading sun.

Kaden kissed my temple and said, "Me too."

We flew until we reached Kaden's warehouse. His once

empty space was now filled with my dresser, bookshelves, and stuffed animals from when I was little. He had moved all the stuff that I needed or cared about here, which made me smile. He really did know me.

I walked over to one of my old, cream-colored teddy bears. The memory of when I'd found it outside my window one night as a little girl replayed in my head. It had always held a special place in my heart, because I thought it was magical, since it had appeared out of nowhere.

Kaden approached me with his wings hidden once more. He smiled at me as he said, "I gave you that one."

I grinned back at him and said, "This one was my favorite."

This made him even happier, and he scooped me into his arms. I let my legs wrap around his waist, and my arms hugged tightly around his neck. I stared into his eyes as I asked, "How did you know they'd gotten to me?"

When we reached the bed, he laid me down on my back, and my head rested softly against the pillow. "I went to check on you. When I saw that no one was at the bookstore and it wasn't locked, I figured you'd left in a hurry. I could only think of one reason why you would have left like that, so I knew they came after you."

I sighed and said, "I was so afraid they were going to hurt you. I just wanted to keep you safe."

He smiled down at me and softly brushed his lips across mine. He leaned back only enough to look into my eyes. "I love you."

I couldn't contain my smile. "I love you too."

His lips met mine again as he pressed our bodies together. He grabbed at my shirt, preparing to take it off. I pulled back to look at him and said, "You know, you promised me that when I was fully recovered, you were going to show me what it was really like." I looked down at myself then back up at him. "I'm recovered."

He grinned at me as he got a gleam in his eye. He leaned down and kissed me with so much passion that it made my head blissfully dizzy. Instead of taking my shirt off, he grabbed the middle of it and pulled the fabric, ripping it from my body. I looked at the torn cloth in his hands as he tossed it aside, smiling down at me.

"That's something else that comes with being an angel," he said with a playful grin. "I'm incredibly strong."

My cheeks flushed as he kissed me again, pinning me to the mattress with his body. He slid out of his pants before tugging mine away too. He wrapped his arms around me and lifted me up to where I was sitting on his lap. My lips parted, letting his tongue glide in. It sent shivers through my body, which seemed to make a fire grow in him.

His wings shot out from his back with a heavy smack, and they beat the air, lifting us up into it. My legs stayed wrapped around his waist as he ripped my bra from me and tossed it to the ground below. He slammed me into the wall high above the bed, and I let out a soft sigh against his lips as his hands started to wander up my inner thighs. When he felt the fabric of my panties, his hands slipped around the hem before tearing them away. Once there was nothing left, he fulfilled his promise, showing me just how much he loved me.

***

I laid there on top of Kaden with my head resting on his chest as it slowly rose and fell. He was twirling a strand of my hair around his finger while smiling down at me. I stared into his perfect eyes, letting a yawn escape me. He grinned wider, and I nuzzled his chest.

"I want it to be like this forever," I said, looking at him again.

"It will be. No more fallen angels. We can finish school, go to college, get married, have a family. We can do it all. Anything that you want."

A warm smile lit my face. A future with Kaden. The idea spurred a warm flutter in my chest. A normal, happy life with him was all I wanted. With him, I was complete. I looked at him and said, "You're right. We can have those things. Someday."

He grinned and kissed me once more. Pulling back, he nodded. "Someday."

Acknowledgements

What a journey. When I started this story back in High School, I figured it would be just another one of my stories that I wrote but never did anything with. Boy, was I wrong! After finishing the story and putting it on the back burner to focus on others, I realized that I wanted to stop *dreaming* of being an author. I wanted to actually *be* an author. Thus, began my journey to publish my first book.

I received so much love and support for my writing from the very beginning. Numerous teachers inspired and encouraged me, so I want to give a huge thanks to all of them. Mr. Huisingh, Mrs. Parker, Mrs. Walsh, and Mr. Martinez; the four of you never stopped pushing me to work hard, and the support you showed my writing was one of my biggest motivators. Thank you so much for believing in me!

My mom and sister were also there for me throughout the entire process. As I would stay up all night writing, my sister would listen to me read what I had so far. She gave me honest feedback, and genuinely cared for the characters. That means a lot, especially since she hates reading. My mom also made sure to read every line of my drafts, letting me know just what she loved and what she didn't. Both of them helped me tremendously, and I owe them both a huge thank you.

There were also loads of people who helped me during the editing and critique phase. One of the biggest helps and blessings were my Beta Readers. Haley and Justine; you guys were the greatest! Thank you so much for sticking with my story and providing such great feedback. I also want to thank my editor, Julie Mianecki. You were so quick and thorough in your edits. I appreciate you helping me fix my mistakes. A huge thank you to Maddie (more commonly known as biggerprint on Instagram). The cover you designed is absolutely stunning, and I am so lucky to have you as a friend. Also, thank you from the bottom of my heart to Lorna Reid! I didn't know the first thing about formatting a book, so you saved me. Thank you for making my book beautiful on every page.

Furthermore, I would like to thank my husband. You are my biggest supporter and encouragement each day. You inspire me and push me to do my very best. Your love plays a huge role in my writing, and it keeps me going, even when I really don't want to. Thank you for being by my side from the beginning of the story until now. I can't wait to have you tag along on my many more writing endeavours in the future.

Lastly, I would like to thank all of you readers. Thank you for taking a chance on me, a new Indie author. I hope I didn't disappoint you, and I'm looking forward to creating more stories for all of you. None of this would've been possible if you hadn't picked up this book and decided to give me and my characters a shot.

Thank you all for believing in me.